Crack Shot

Bert Johnson was looking for a job, but when he strayed onto Curly Bar 6 land he was braced by old Shorty and taken to the Old Man. Now Bert was an Oklahoman and as tough as they came, with skills to match the best. Perhaps the Old Man saw all that, but in any event Bert was soon on the payroll. There was trouble on the range with several men having been bushwhacked and the sheriff was getting nowhere.

Then Bert discovered his partner had been jailed and accused of the bushwhacking. That was when Johnson really made his presence felt. No man would stop him now. By God, he'd find the killer – and accomplish his secret mission of revenge.

Crack Shot

Jake Ross

A Black Horse Western

ROBERT HALE · LONDON

© Vic J. Hanson 1951, 2003
First hardcover edition 2003
Originally published in paperback as
Bushwacker! by V. Joseph Hanson

ISBN 0 7090 7280 5

Robert Hale Limited
Clerkenwell House
Clerkenwell Green
London EC1R 0HT

Typeset by
Derek Doyle & Associates, Liverpool.
Printed and bound in Great Britain by
Antony Rowe Limited, Wiltshire

ONE

The man in the red shirt halted his mount on the crest of the rise. It was late afternoon and the sun had lost much of its power. It shone benignly on the valley below, bringing a golden glow to the acre-upon-acre of grassland, the sturdy cluster of ranch buildings, the corrals, the herds of grazing beef, the mountains blue and hazy on the opposite horizon.

It was a sight to gladden men's hearts, but the face of the lone horseman did not show one flicker of emotion. Although he was young his was the sort of face that seemed ageless: healthy with a brown flush of blood, clean-shaven, square, unwrinkled, the eyes light-blue and curiously inward-looking, the mouth tight, the nose a little snub. The long hair, flowing from beneath the battered Stetson, was brittle and yellow like dried corn.

The body was squarely-built too, loaded with muscle, the sweat-stained red check shirt tight across the shoulders, chest and upper arms, the thighs bulging in greasy black chaps.

Above the open neck of the shirt showed the square

top of a flannel vest, grimy with long wear; above this the black kerchief, tied tightly, looked little more than a shoestring bow. The neck it encircled, the colour of old mahogany, was columned with muscle.

The man's short leather jacket was slung across his saddle pommel with his lariat, next to the polished butt of the rifle in the long boot. Across his flat belly was a thick leather belt with a silver clasp and atop that, looping across the right-hand hip, a loaded gunbelt. The holster was shapeless and shiny with grease below the walnut butt of a Colt. The butt was ridged to give a better grip. The holster was tied down to the trouser-leg by a whang-string which ran beneath the flared chaps. Riding-boots, badly worn and scuffed lopsided on the high heels rested in stirrups of leather and plaited horse-hair.

The horse was a black stallion, huge and powerful, shiny with careful grooming. Its saddle was chased in silver, bridle and reins sprinkled with studs of the same metal, winking in the sunlight.

From his pants-pocket the man took out a bandanna of the same hue as his shirt. He cuffed back his Stetson and wiped his streaming brow. Then he ran the cloth down both sides of the horse's neck.

With a pressure of his knees he eased the black gently down the slope and, as they began to level out again, set him at a canter. He was making for the grove of trees he had noticed from up on the ridge, remembering the gleam he had seen among them, as of sun shining on water. His horse's eagerness as they got nearer proved to him that his surmise had been correct. He gave the black his head, leaning over the mane as the powerful beast broke into a gallop.

They drove into the grove at breakneck speed; the lower branches of the trees, which were very close together, plucking at man and beast as they thundered past. The man ducked to avoid a sturdy bough.

'Easy,' he said. At the sound of his voice the horse immediately slowed down, his nostrils quivering.

The trees broke away from them suddenly and they were in a tiny glade. Long lush grass; a brighter splash here and there of wild flowers; a shrub of white briar; a sheen of water. The man dismounted from the horse and led him down to the edge of the small water-hole, where he let the horse drink but did not immediately do so himself. He looked all around him, then he looked at the ground at his feet. The grass ended a few yards from the water's edge and here was clayey ground. It had been trampled hard and was pitted here and there, but if there was any spoor the man found it hard to define.

He got down on his hands and knees and put his face to the water. He sipped slowly. He straightened his body, took out his red bandanna and dipped it into the water. He wrung it out then he laved his face and neck with the damp cloth. He took off his hat and ran the wadded cloth around the leather sweat-band. He kept back his long hair with his hand and replaced the Stetson.

As he rose he made a clicking noise with his tongue. The horse's ears pricked up and he turned his head towards his master. Then he moved closer.

The man reached upwards and took the water canteen which dangled beside the war-bag on the cantle, below the tightly-rolled slicker-covered bedroll. He shucked out the cork, letting it dangle on its string, and dipped the bottle into the water. When it was filled to his liking he recorked it.

He was reaching up to replace it on the saddle when a gun barked flatly. The bottle was smashed out of his hand into the water once more. His head swivelled and he went for his gun.

'Hold it, yuh durn' fool!' said a voice.

He remained with his hand clawed an inch above the gun and looked at the bow-legged little man who stood in the edge of the trees.

The little man grinned. 'Good job I'm a crack-shot,' he said. 'I might've blown your head off.'

The other looked at the water; his canteen had sunk beneath it.

'Drilled it clean, uh?' said the little man conversationally. 'Raise your hands, pardner, an' get up slowly.'

The other one did as he was told. The little man admired the set of him, watching him warily at the same time. He said: 'Which way did you ride in, pardner?'

The young man pointed.

The little man jerked a thumb. 'If you'd 'a' come in from the side there you'd 'a' seen the notice.'

'What notice?'

'Oh, you do talk then? The notice which says this is Curly Bar 6 land for Curly Bar 6 folks, an' everybody else keep out.'

'That's no reason f'r the gun-play. I didn't see any notice.'

'It was li'l Ernest here.' He patted the long barrel of

the old Peacemaker Colt which bulged enormously in his small horny fist. 'He don't get enough exercise – he ain't done a thing since he polished off a prairie-rabbit coupla days ago. The Ol' Man likes us to keep saddle tramps off'n his territory but he don't like us shooting off guns all over the place. Kind of a queer cuss, the Ol' Man.'

'What ol' man's that?'

The little man's grin threatened to split his wizened face in twain. 'I'm askin' the questions! What's your handle? Where'd yuh come from? What yuh doin' here?'

'Muh name's Bert. I'm lookin' for a job.'

The way the little man managed to grin so widely and talk so much all at the same time was a minor phenomenon. 'Bert, uh? I once knew an English feller by the name o' Bert – wouldn't be any relative o' yourn would he?'

'No!'

'I was jist askin'. So yuh lookin' for a job, uh? Cowhand?'

'What do I look like?'

'Yeh, I see what yuh mean. You're takin' this purty coolly young feller.'

'The way things are I cain't do nothin' else. If I get a-holt of yuh I'll break you in two.'

The little man spat drily. 'Pah! Injun talk! Lower your arms slowly an' drop your gun-belt.'

The young man obeyed.

'Now hook your toe under it and kick it towards me.'

Again the young man complied. The belt, with its full quota of cartridges and the heavy gun, landed with a thud a few yards in front of him.

The little man swayed forward, his legs like two halves of a hoop. 'Don't try any tricks,' he said. With a swift motion he bent and scooped up the gun-belt, then he stepped back again.

'Now, Bert, there's one question you ain't answered. Where'd yuh come from?'

'Mebbe I'll answer that to the one who gives me a job – an' mebbe I won't.'

'Not so fast, young feller. I ain't heerd the Ol' Man say he wants any new fish . . . Anyway, he mightn't like the cut of your jib. I ain't even sure whether I like the cut of your jib muhself. You'd better mind your manners or I'm liable to run you off without any more sayso from anybody.'

'Hurry up an' make up your mind. I'm gettin' stiff standin' here. Also I could do with some chucker.'

'Wal, ain't you a forthright young skunk?' The little man pranced forward again, moving around to the other side of the horse. The beast stood motionless. The little man reached across the saddle for the rifle in the boot the other side.

He had to get on tip-toes and stretch his arm. The gun in his other hand was poked over the top of the saddle and pointed at the young man's head.

'I'll let you ride but I ain't taking any chances.'

'You talk too much,' said Bert. He whistled sharply between his teeth. The horse swung his head around quickly and reared towards its master. His back legs bent and the little man, thrown off balance, slid down over his rump. He cursed and the gun in his hand went off. Bert's hat was whisked from his head, did a neat parabola and landed in the water; it

10

floated there sedately on its brim.

Shorty scrambled on all fours, the barrel of his gun imbedded in the soft clay. The young man leapt forward and put his foot on the back of Shorty's neck. Screaming curses the little man was shoved on to his stomach. The curses bubbled inarticulately in his throat as his face was pressed into the mud.

'You little jackass,' said Bert. 'You might've killed me.'

He bent and retrieved Shorty's gun and thrust it into his own belt. He took his foot off the man's neck, then he turned and picked up his own gun-belt. As he fastened it around his waist he watched Shorty slowly rise to his feet, raking the mud out of his eyes, spluttering and still cursing. His hand moved swiftly as the little man put his own muddied one into his pocket. But Shorty was only after his kerchief and Bert's hand came away from his gun once more.

'Where's your hoss?'

Shorty looked up with mottled face and jerked a thumb. 'In the trees,' he said. 'I was there when you came in. I saw yuh up on the rise an' I waited.'

'My hoss was mad-thirsty or he'd've spotted yuh. Get movin'. Get your hoss.'

Shorty finished wiping himself and replaced his kerchief. He turned and bumbled off. His legs seemed more bowed than ever. Bert, his thumbs hooked into his belt, followed him.

He got closer to the little man. He took his gun out of its holster and Shorty's gun out of his belt too. He reached forward and dropped Shorty's gun back into its rightful place. The little man halted. Bert said:

11

'Keep movin'. An' don't reach for that iron – I've got you covered. I'm bein' mighty nice to yuh. I oughta blow your haid off.'

Shorty, grinning again, looked over his shoulder. His grin died. The younker's queer light-blue eyes gave him the creeps. He had an idea Bert had a very good reason for being 'mighty nice'.

His horse was a raw-boned little brown cow-pony with a white blaze across his face. 'Get up on him,' said Bert. 'Turn around an' ride on back to the clearing.'

It was Shorty's turn to do as he was told. A few moments later the two men rode out of the glade the opposite end to which Bert had entered it.

They rode side by side with a few yards of space between them. Bert had sheathed his gun once more but he had said:

'If you want to try and draw there's nothin' to stop yuh. But I'm warnin' yuh – I'm fast.'

For once Shorty did not say anything. He merely grinned again. His mud-bath did not seem to have dampened his spirits a whole lot. The sun was sinking a little, a faint breeze blew the grass against the horses' fetlocks with a little 'shock-shicking' sound. Making their way through clusters of prime steers who watched them placidly and incuriously with their big milky eyes, the two men made for the cluster of ranch buildings at the lowest point of the plain.

Shorty and his little pony were dwarfed by the young man and his mount, and the little fellow looked upwards as he spoke.

'That's a mighty handsome beast. I ain't seen one like that in years.' He wagged his head and patted the neck of his own mount. 'But I'll settle for muh own little cayuse. They're the best kind to have in this territory.'

'Blackie can do anythin' a pesky runt of a cow-pony can do.' For the first time since they had met Bert sounded a little peeved.

Shorty's lips quirked again. Here was a queer cuss indeed. He was shot at twice and he didn't turn a hair – but let a man slight his horse and he acted fair to blow his top. Shorty found himself getting a little annoyed at this – more annoyed than when he suffered the humiliation of having his face rubbed in the mud: he had asked for that anyway. But who did this galoot think he was – him and his fancy horse?

Shorty's thoughts were brought to a stop by an abrupt and painful shock. Something like an iron-hard spiked fist hit him a terrific blow on the shoulder. An involuntary cry burst from his lips and he felt himself falling. He thought he heard the flat echoes of a shot and then he hit the ground and things became hazy.

Hoofs thundered and, rising on one elbow he realized that the other man was no longer beside him. That must be him, that vague shape there, getting hazier all the time. The dirty skunk was running away!

Shorty took his other hand away from his shoulder and looked at it as if he had never seen it before. He wiped it carefully on his trousers, then he took his kerchief out of his pocket, wadded it and pressed it to his shoulder. Things began to whirl around him then. He cursed and let himself fall on to his back.

The sound of drumming hoofs impinged itself on his consciousness once more. Coming nearer! The skunk

13

was coming back to finish off his job!

Shorty writhed over on to his side and reached for his gun. The big black horse loomed over him. A voice said:

'Hold it, old-timer.'

Bert landed on both feet. Shorty cursed him and pointed the gun. Bert leapt, rolled beside him, wrested the weapon out of his hand.

'You fool,' he said. 'Bushwhacker – I chased him – he'd got a start.'

'I might've known it,' said Shorty. 'Sorry.' Then he fainted.

TWO

When he came to his senses he was lying on his cot in the bunkhouse. He was alone. From the kitchen came the cheerful clatter of pots and pans. Shorty felt his shoulder. It had been roughly bandaged and it hurt like hell. He opened his mouth and bellowed: 'Nolly.'

From the direction of the kitchen, after the clattering ceased, a plaintive voice said: 'I'm coming.'

The door opened and a huge black-jowled man stooped his way through.

'As if I ain't got enough to do, you hafta go an' get yuhself shot. Not even daid like the other two, either.'

'That ain't funny, Nolly.'

'The big man sighed. 'No, I guess it ain't. What can I do f'r yuh, Shorty?'

'Information is what I want. What happened to that yaller-haired young cuss?'

'He brought you in. Said he'd met you in the glade then while you was both on the way to the ranch you got bushwhacked. Slug just missed him. He chased the skunk, but he'd got too big a start. Slim met you – he thought the stranger had done it at fust. I ran outa the

15

kitchen – I thought there was gonna be some gunplay – you know how fiery Slim is. Anyway, he put two an' two together mighty quick – like I said myself, if the stranger 'ud shot yuh he wouldn't have brought you in, would he? Anyway, you was hit by a high-powered slug from one o' them new-type Winchesters. It's lodged somewhere under the bone. Slim sent for the doc – he should be here any minute now.'

'What's the Ol' Man say about this?'

'He's bin in here. He's jumping mad – an' mighty worried, too, if you ask me.' Nolly wagged his head sagely.

'I guess you're lucky, Shorty – that's the first time that galoot didn't make a finishing job.'

'Mebbe it wasn't the same one. Blake an' Simkins were both shot in the back – with a Colt forty-five.'

'The stranger carries a Colt forty-five.'

'F'r Pete's sake – so do I an' a good many more o' the boys,' Shorty snorted. 'I suppose purty soon we'll have Sheriff Bighead here as well.'

'Yuh know the Ol' Man allus says he'll do his own investigatin'. But I guess the doc's obleeged tuh bring the law along in a case like this.'

'He'll look at me an' he'll flap his goatee but he won't get any nearer to finding out who killed Blake an' Simkins.'

'I'm surprised at you, Shorty, picking up that stranger after all what's happened around here lately.'

'I'll tell you all about that later.' Shorty's face was whitening. 'Get me a shot o' somep'n, Nolly. This shoulder feels like somebody's runnin' a brandin'-iron across it.'

Nolly turned, stooped and vanished. He reappeared a few seconds later with a tin mug full of whiskey. Shorty took it gratefully.

'Where's the stranger now?' he said. 'Calls hisself Bert. Fust Bert I've met for years.'

'He went into the office with Slim an' the Ol' Man a coupla minutes ago.'

'He wants a job . . . The Ol' Man 'ull put him through his paces.'

Shorty sighed, and lay back on his pillows. 'It's kinda peaceful here. Better'n ridin' out an' maybe gettin' shot at again.'

'You're too durned self-satisfied.'

'Wal, you said yuhself I'm lucky I ain't in a long box. I reckon I owe that bushwhacker a debt o' thanks for jest pinkin' me this-away so I can rest up nice an' easy while other poor cusses sweat an' toil in the blazin' sun—' Shorty's voice ran out, his face crinkled again with pain. 'I'll be a whole lot better when the slug's out.'

'Lay down an' don't talk so much.'

'Ooh, listen tuh that feller, will yuh? – the champee-un hog-caller hisself—'

'Brother,' said Nolly. 'As a chinwagger I bow to your superior speed and choice elocution.'

'Get back in your kitchen an' read some more o' your high falutin' books,' said Shorty.

The huge cook grinned and went. 'I'll bring yuh some chow,' he called over his shoulder. Shorty lay back and began to curse softly, and with admirable versatility, beneath his breath.

The man who called himself Bert stood before the desk and looked across it into the face of Cal Summerson, who everybody called 'The Ol' Man', and with his long grey hair and walrus moustache, his lined face and his habit of continually chewing tobacco, he lived up to his name. He was huge and stooping and craggy and there was something deep in his eyes that made men wonder about him, fear him, and yet sometimes pity him.

The furrows in his brow were deeper than ever now as he looked at the newcomer and the taller young man beside him, dark and whiplike and called Slim Grady.

'The name's Johnson, suh,' said the blocky young man. 'Bert Johnson.'

'What do yuh do?'

'Anythin' round a ranch, suh.'

'Oh, jack of all trades, uh. I've seen your sort before. Good at none.' The Old Man's voice was a rasping peevish bark.

'You could try me, suh.'

'Yeh, I could at that. Where'd you come from?'

'Oklahoma, suh.'

'What yuh doin' in this part o' the country?'

'Jest ridin'. Figured I'd find me some new sights, new faces.'

The Old Man's smouldering eyes raked Bert Johnson up and down, noting the strong expressionless face, the queer-looking eyes, the build.

'You don't look the sort to be gallivantin'.'

'I ain't, suh. If I get me a good job in these parts I'll stick.'

'I don't want any grasshoppers on my spread. If you

18

start for me you don't get no pay till the end of the month.'

'Thank you, suh.'

'Not so fast. I ain't said I've hired yuh yet. You on the run?'

'If I was I wouldn't've brought in that wounded man, knowing the law 'ud get here sooner or later.'

The Old Man laughed: it was an unlovely sound.

'Didn't you feel like hightailin' it out of here when you got shot at. An' ain't you curious what the shootin' 'ud be about?'

'No to both counts. I guess if I start to work here – an' if there's an explanation for the shootin' – I'll get to hear about it sooner or later.'

'Everythin' happens to you sooner or later, don't it, cowboy,' sneered the Old Man. 'What d'yuh think, Slim?'

'I can use him if he's as good as he thinks he is,' said Slim. 'But you're the boss. Do we hire him or do I toss him out?'

Bert Johnson did not say anything but he looked at Slim with his light blue eyes with that curious inward look. Their lack of emotion was as potent as any flush of rage.

Slim smiled thinly. The Old Man said: 'Looks like you two'ull get along fine. All right, Johnson, you're hired. But if you're a flop you'll go off'n this spread a damsight quicker'n you came on. Slim 'ull show you the ropes. He's ramrod here an' what he tells you to do, you do. Savvy?'

'Yes, sur. Thanks – suh.'

The two young men left the office and walked across

the yard in the dust. As they passed the corral a lone silver grey stallion rolled his eyes wickedly at them over the fence and snorted a challenge.

'Ever done any hoss-breakin', Bert?' said Slim. There was a bantering note in his voice.

'Some.'

Slim jerked a thumb. 'There's a crittur you can have a go at later on.'

'What's the matter, ain't you got a wrangler here who can break him?'

The stranger's tone was as level as ever; Slim gave him a sideways glance. 'He's a killer.'

'I'll have a go at him later.'

Slim was about to make a snappy rejoinder when a crash from over by the stables made him stop and whirl in his tracks. A lad came through the stable doors at breakneck speed, tripped over his own feet and fell on his face.

Slim began to laugh at the sight. As he ran forward rage struggled with his mirth. The stranger's black horse stood in the stable doors and looked around him. Then he began to prance forward daintily towards the fallen stableboy. The lad got up, threw a terrified glance over his shoulder and bolted again. He cannoned headlong into Slim Grady and they both went down.

Behind them Bert Johnson shouted: 'Get back, Blackie. Get back in there.'

The horse had an expression on its face which was suspiciously like a leer. However it turned obediently and trotted back into the gloom of the stables.

A ripple of laughter from the right of Bert made him turn. A girl in riding-costume stood there. Her head was thrown back and her jet-black hair flowed over her shoulders.

Bert came to himself and started forward to help his contemporary and the stable-lad to their feet. The girl continued to laugh.

Slim was already on his pins and helping the lad up. He turned and glared at Bert.

'You—' He stopped then as if hearing the laughter for the first time. He did not turn but now his expression had gone almost murderous.

The stable-lad swayed. 'I wouldn't go in there again for all the gold in the hills – not while that black crittur's there. He's just plumb crazy. I'd hardly laid a finger on him 'fore he tried to bite my haid off.'

The girl was coming nearer but, at the last sally, she stopped and once more went off into gales of laughter. 'You know I'm gentle with my hosses, Slim.'

'I'm sorry,' put in Bert Johnson. 'I forgot to tell you that Blackie won't let anybody else groom him an' feed him 'cept me.'

'Why the heck didn't you say so. He might've killed me.'

'He wouldn't. He ain't vicious – jest a little rough at times.'

'Rough!' said the stable-lad explosively. He stood straddle-legged, arms akimbo, and glowered at the stranger.

Bert Johnson returned his look impassively. He was not looking at him and he was looking through him – all at the same time. Something like a shudder ran through the lad's narrow frame. He dropped his hands and turned away.

The stranger said: 'Jest go to the stable doors an' call Blackie. He'll come. He won't hurt yuh now he knows I'm here.'

'Call him yuhself.'

Bert Johnson whistled shrilly between his teeth. The stable-lad got out of the way fearfully as the black horse pranced into view.

The girl had gotten over her laughing fit. She came nearer.

'Aren't you hurt, Slim?' she said.

'Wouldn't seem to make a heck of a lot of difference to some folks if I was,' said Slim like a sullen child. 'I'm all in one piece I guess.'

'Poor old Slim,' said the girl, her red lips pouting, a sudden caressing note in her voice. 'But you did look funny rollin' on the ground with Bill. I thought for a minute you were fightin' again.'

'Things happen around here that are liable to make a man fighting mad.' Slim threw a dark look in Johnson's direction.

The new man seemed oblivious of it: he was stroking his horse and the big black was nudging him playfully. When he did look up Slim was looking at the girl again. Her figure was almost voluptuous in the tight riding-habit she wore. Hers was a lusty Spanish-type of beauty, she looked an ideal mate for any man of the outdoors. Johnson said:

'I'll take him into the stables an' fix him up muhself, Slim.'

He led the horse past the two of them and the girl turned her head and gave him a slanting look from under her lashes. Bert tipped his hat gravely and went on with the horse. Slim scowled. He said softly:

'Do you hafta give the eye to every unattached ranny who comes along?'

'I merely looked at the man. I've never seen him before.'

'That's what I mean.'

'Oh, Slim, you're incorrigible.'

'I don't know what that fancy word means but the same to you – in spades.'

'You're childish.' The girl tossed her head and turned away from him.

He watched her flounce away, tapping her thigh with her quirt, her hips waggling. A dull flush mounted from his neckline up over his face. He strode towards the stable.

Bert Johnson was grooming his horse, while the black had his nose in a bag of oats. Bill, the stable-lad, sat in a corner out of harm's way and watched the proceedings.

Hot words bubbled on Slim's lips but remained unsaid. He was ramrod of the Curly Bar 6 – the Ol' Man would have the pants off'n him if he started a brawl in front of the stable-lad. He said:

'When you've finished here, Johnson, come down to the bunkhouse for some chow.'

'Right.'

Slim turned sharply out of the stables. A few of the men were riding in. They greeted him.

The ranch house, which was the larger, double-storeyed central pile of the little wood-built settlement, lay beyond the bunkhouse. As the men filed into the latter Slim passed them and went on.

The girl was standing in the doorway of the smaller stables beside the ranch house. She beckoned him. He quickened his pace, swaying a little on his high-heeled boots. She backed into the shadows and he followed her.

She came to him as soon as he crossed the threshold, leaned her head on his breast and put her arms around him. 'Don't be mad at me, Slim. I hate it when you're mad at me.'

'I ain't mad at you, Luella.'

'You acted that way.'

'You shouldn't've laughed. That got my goat. An' that new feller does – I'll have to take him down a peg or two. What authority d'yuh think I'm gonna have over the men if you laugh at me in front of them. . . ?'

'I couldn't help it, Slim – you looked so funny.'

'All right. I heard that . . .'

'Honey, don't be that way.' She nestled against him and lifted her face.

Slim's arms tightened, his face went taut. He bent and kissed her hard, brutally. She strained against him and gave back all she got.

When they had finished they were both panting a little. She said: 'Now, you silly boy, come in and have tea with us.'

'Not me. The Ol' Man's in one of his bad moods today.'

The girl's eyes flashed and she stood away from him. Her bosom heaved in the tight shirt-waist she wore beneath her open riding-coat.

'So I've got to bear the brunt of it alone?'

'All right, don't go off half-cocked about it. Anyway, I ain't married to yuh yet.'

24

'Nor you damwell won't be,' she stormed past him.

His face changed, he looked alarmed; a little cowed as if she had suddenly lashed him across the face with her quirt. He darted forward and as she went through the doorway grabbed her arm and pulled her back into the gloom. Behind them horses moved restlessly. She was pressed against him again and she smiled like she always did when she knew she'd have her own way. She always got her own way.

'I didn't mean it, honey,' he said. 'You know that. It's only that I've had the Ol' Man on my back nearly all day. An' you know how awkward he can be at times—'

'You'll come with me. You'll do it for me, won't you? You ain't scared o' the Ol' Man—?'

'Naw, I ain't scared o' the Ol' Man. I'll come in with yuh. Though how he's gonna act I don't know. I guess he's seen enough of my ugly mug.'

The girl was kittenish. That way she was more seductive than ever: she could twist a man around her little finger. 'Oh, Slim, you know you're not ugly. You're the handsomest man on the ranch—'

'Handsomer than that new fellah?'

'Don't bring that up again. I hardly looked at him. I wouldn't know if he was cross-eyed.'

Slim smiled then. 'All right, I'll risk the Ol' Man. Anythin' for you, *chiquita*.'

She caught hold of his face and kissed him hard. She said: 'Father's obleeged to be nice to his prospective son-in-law – knowing how much his only daughter loves her dark an' handsome Slim.'

She caught hold of his hand and pulled him out of the stable.

Slim drew his hand away. 'Luella. The men—'

She walked a little way in front of him then, and he admired the sturdy sway of her hips. When Luella wasn't acting up she was a proper lady, and a sturdy frontierswoman to boot.

Looking through his kitchen window, Nolly the cook said, 'Oh, Romeo, Romeo—' He made a grand flourish with his skillet then cursed as a blob of grease fell on his bare arm.

THREE

The men's quarters of the Curly Bar 6 consisted of a bunkhouse and a mess-hut. The latter was reached by crossing the bunkhouse and going through another door. Nolly's kitchen was a low, narrow lean-to running the whole length of both rooms and with a door each end, one leading into the bunkhouse, the other into the mess.

When the new man, Bert, came out of the stables he could not see Slim Grady so he went across to the place he knew to be the bunkhouse and entered it.

Shorty was sitting up in his bunk digging into a bowl of stew Nolly had given him. He looked up.

'Howdy, Bert,' he said without warmth. 'You get a job?'

'Yeh. How yuh feelin'?'

'Not bad. Thanks for bringing me in.'

'Forget it.'

'Sorry I hadda throw down on yuh. If you're gonna be a member of this outfit I guess you'll purty soon find out why I had to do it. Don't ask me to tell yuh.'

'I ain't askin'.'

'Jest tellin' yuh thassall.' The garrulous Shorty tried to give one of his eloquent shrugs and almost howled with the pain it caused him.

'Yuh don't bear no grudge?' he said.

'Nope. No grudge.'

'If you want some chow go through that door. Hark at 'em – like a lot o' jackals. Best get in before they gobble it all up.' Shorty raised his voice. 'Hey, Nolly! New customer!'

Bert passed through into the mess-hut to meet a battery of eyes. He noted a bare space along the bench and made for it. He straddled the bench, got right over, and sat down.

'Howdy,' said his right-hand neighbour. The left-hand one maintained a stubborn silence.

'Howdy,' said the newcomer. The eyes were taken away from him now and the steady sound of champing and guzzling was resumed from all sides.

'Name's Gil Pendexter,' said the right-hand man.

'Bert Johnson.'

'Glad to know yuh, Bert.' Pendexter reached over and tapped the left-hand man. 'Pat, this is the new ranny; calls hisself Bert Johnson.'

The redhaired man with shoulders as bulky as Johnson's looked up from under bushy brows. His eyes were little and choleric in a brick-red face sprinkled with yellow specks of freckles. 'Howdy,' he grunted.

Pendexter said: 'Pat's an Irishman. Right now he's in one of his moods. He's a dead ringer for the Ol' Man. When the Ol' Man has a mood Pat has one too. Mebbe he's practisin' for when the Ol' Man leaves him the ranch in his will.'

28

The man the other side of Pendexter began to laugh. The Irishman turned around. In his hand was a fork. He reached across in front of Johnson and jabbed at Pendexter's hand where it lay supine on the edge of the table.

The sharp steel prongs penetrated the flesh and the Irishman pressed on hard until the blood began to spurt. A cry of agony was forced from Pendexter's lips. He got to his feet but his hand remained pinned to the table.

The Irishman took the fork away. Pendexter swayed, then crashed over backwards.

The Irishman began to laugh. It was a sneering, baying sound. He looked at the newcomer by his side and laughed harder. Johnson looked back and then he turned on the bench and helped the white-faced Pendexter to his feet.

Pendexter swayed for a moment then he launched himself at the Irishman. Pat turned and struck low with one huge fist. It sank into Pendexter's middle. The man gulped horribly and doubled up. As he lurched forward Pat hit him again, flush on the point of the jaw. The big man was still sitting in his seat, his body half-turned. He used his right hand only, his left still held the fork.

Pendexter hit the wall with a crash; he remained upright for a split second like a butterfly on a pin, then slowly slid to a sitting position. His head lolled on one side, his mouth open, his eyes closed.

Everybody gaped; nobody moved or said anything. Then Pat began to laugh once more.

He looked at the newcomer, laughed in his face.

29

'That's the way to treat 'em when they don't mind their manners,' he said and slapped Johnson on the back.

The young man did not bend beneath the blow. He looked at Pat and he said: 'Don't ever do that again.'

Pat stopped laughing. His bovine red face crinkled with perplexity. He said: ' 'Tain't nothin' tuh you what I do to Pendexter. He asked for it.'

'I ain't talkin' about Pendexter. Maybe he did ask for it – I dunno. I'm tellin' yuh never to slap me again like that.'

Pat's little eyes widened. 'Slap yuh,' he said. 'A little friendly slap like that.' His voice rose. 'Everybody saw me give him that little friendly slap, didn't they?'

Nobody spoke – except Johnson. 'It wasn't intended to be a friendly slap. It was hard – it was meant to impress on me – seein' as I'm a new fish – that you think you're cock of the bunkhouse or somethin' or other.' Johnson's tones were utterly flat. They did not change one jot as he looked around. 'He does think he's cock o' the roost don't he?'

The voice that answered did not come from anyone at the tables but from Nolly as he came in from the kitchen.

'Yeh, he thinks he's cock o' the roost, all right. I've told him before not to pick fights near to my kitchen. One o' these days I'm gonna cut him in half with a meat cleaver.'

Pat rose, his attention taken away from the upstart of a newcomer. Nolly came nearer. 'Sit down, You mad Irishman,' he said. ' 'Fore I pour this stew all over yuh.'

Again Pat's face crinkled with perplexity. Then he sat down.

30

'Touchy, ain't yuh?' jeered Nolly. 'What did Pendexter say – that your mother was an Irish washerwoman?' Pat growled deep in his throat and rose again. Nolly balanced the huge plate of stew and looked at him meaningly. Pat sat down again. Holly put the plate of stew down in front of Johnson.

'Tuck intuh that, son. An' if you've got any complaints pop into the kitchen an' let me know.'

'I shouldn't,' said a man across the table. 'Last man who complained about Nolly's grub vanished off'n the face o' the earth.'

'An' we had meat pie f'r weeks afterwards,' said another one.

The two long tables rocked with laughter. Pat the Irishman's bray rang above it all. While this was going on Gil Pendexter rose shakily to his feet. The glance he shot at the big Irishman was murderous, but Pat did not seem to notice it.

However, when Pendexter regained his seat the Irishman looked at him and said: 'I'm sorry I laced yuh, Gil. Mighty sorry I am. I don't know me own strength. I was in a black mood – you was right – an' I lost me temper. The black mood's gone now. I'll make it up to yuh, Gil me boy. Shore I will . . .'

Pendexter said nothing. He swallowed painfully as he took a gulp of stew.

Johnson intercepted the Irishman's gaze. The little eyes were anxious, the red forehead furrowed.

'Shore, I am mighty sorry I hit the feller, misther. Don't you believe that?'

'I believe it,' said Johnson briefly and turned back to his plate.

Pat shook his head dolefully. Again he tried to catch Pendexter's eye. But the latter was nursing his wounds and his hate as he bent over his plate.

The living-room of the Curly Bar 6 always had a depressing effect on the volatile Slim. It was a long low place with a huge brick fire-place at one end, the only collection of bricks in the whole spread, and a door at the other. Another smaller door at the side led into the kitchen. Opposite it was the only window which, besides the usual drapes, was covered entirely by mesh curtains – because the Old Man affirmed he didn't want any ignorant cowpokes gawping into his living quarters.

The long dining-table ran almost the whole length of the room, except for a space by the fire and another by the door. It had a depressing feudal appearance and the man of the house, with time-honoured custom, sat at the head of it – the fire end. The Old Man always complained of the cold. Even in the height of summer he was muffled up – as the boys said: like Father Christmas. And, in his lighter moments, Slim was wont to affirm that the Old Man sat with his backside up the chimney.

So, except on the rare occasions when they had visitors, or Slim dined with them, this hawk-like old-timer, with the huge body going to seed and the haunted eyes, sat supreme at the head of his board and his daughter sat halfway down the table on his right-hand side.

Slim often wondered how a lusty, beautiful girl managed to stick it through the long nights alone in the house with the brooding old man – except for the housekeeper, who had a room of her own at the back. After her chores were done she was not allowed in the forepart of the house. She cooked the evening meal and Luella fetched it from the kitchen and served it herself.

Luella sat beneath the portrait of her mother which the Old Man had had painted one time back East when both of them were young. Even this exemplified his sombre taste, for it was displayed in a massive black frame and the artist, probably under his patron's instructions, had made plenty of use of shadows to gain his effect. Luella's mother had been a very beautiful woman. She loomed out of the picture like beauty incarnate – but also, in the eyes of Slim, who had never known her – a little evil.

At times Luella reminded Slim of that portrait and then he almost hated her – while she doubly fascinated him. She was all woman – maddeningly so – and she knew it! As she sat beneath the portrait that evening, and the Old Man brooded at the head of the board, Slim cast surreptitious glances at the girl and the picture in the half-gloom behind her – a gloom shot here and there by glimmers of a dying sun. Luella's dark flamboyant beauty was intensified by the wine coloured dress she wore which shimmered here and there as it caught the light. It was the lowest cut garment Slim had ever seen her in and showed an expanse of plump, olive-white flesh which made his heart pound to look upon.

Her hair was now elaborately curled: it was long and heavy and glossy and she seemed to be able to do anything with it. It was pinned up Spanish-fashion with a huge tortoiseshell comb studded with stones which Slim knew to be real diamonds. There was something very like it in the hair of the figure in the portrait above – maybe it was the very same comb.

From time to time Luella intercepted Slim's glances from under her long lowered lashes and sent him coquettish ones in return. She was teasing him – and she maddened him. The Old Man, champing slowly, seemed oblivious of either of them.

Above Luella the portrait almost glowered on the little assembly. The mother had been very beautiful – with the full-blown Spanish type of beauty; she had been the daughter of a Mexican Don. Slim had the idea she must have been a man-eater: she had certainly left her mark on the Old Man. Once the young ramrod had come into that room during the day when the sun was blazing on the picture. It had been something he would not easily forget: the artist had caught the full power of that exotic woman and put it on the canvas for all time. It was there in the little sideways glint of the big dark eyes – Luella looked like that sometimes – the arrogant set of the head, the curve of the full red lips in the little half-smile. The gown was low-cut, of a deep red colour. The artist had cut off the picture just below the bosom of the woman. That was all he needed: she was there, personified.

Slim often wondered whether the real woman had been like that. The Old Man never spoke of her. She was part of his past life – he had roamed then. Where had he met and married that exotic beauty? Slim had never seen a woman like that this far west. The nearest thing to her was, of course, Luella – she was so very much like her at times – but Luella was not so sultry-looking, she seemed more virile, she was a lusty young frontierswoman. Slim was crazy about her, filled always with the terrible fear that he might lose her, madly jealous of any other man who looked at her.

He remembered the first day he had arrived at the Curly Bar 6. That was seven years ago. He had been a younker of nineteen, an orphan brought up by an uncle, among steers and horses all the time. The uncle had died and the younker roamed.

The Old Man was shorthanded and he gave Slim a job. His bunch were a rough lot in those days – there weren't many of them left on the spread now.

Slim remembered seeing Luella for the first time, a gangling kid riding a fractious colt in the corral and conducting herself like a real bronco-buster. He had watched her grow suddenly into a beautiful woman and had fallen in love with her. She had played around with him, then suddenly it seemed she was in love too, and they were engaged and he, who had proved himself the best cowhand of the bunch – had seen them come and seen them go – was boss of them all, a ramrod at twenty-two. That proved the Old Man had faith in him – though you wouldn't think so the way the ol' buzzard acted. And though he had given his permission to the engagement – Luella was free, white and over twenty-one anyway – he never passed any opinion as to what he thought about the arrangement.

He never asked either of them when they intended to get married. Luella herself seemed to be in no hurry – though Slim, the many times he had been so deadly afraid of losing her, tried to push things. There were too many men around on a big spread like the Curly

Bar 6 – and although many of them were ornery old mossy-horns, or galoots who had wives in the nearby town of Sorrowful Creek, there were bound to be a few hardboiled presentable young men who chased after every pretty girl they saw, whether she was engaged to some other fellow or not. And particularly so when the gel in question had a roving eye.

There had never been harm in any of it – so far as Slim knew anyway – Luella was just a natural-born flirt, probably took after her mother before her, that woman who had burned herself out so young. Slim had seen them come and seen them go – men that was, lusty young men with devilment in their hearts. Slim had had to fight some of them – sometimes he lost but most times he won. He was good – he knew that. He remembered Sonny Jackson, Pete Lous, Ginger Fredericks, Al Morganson – and that sky-pilot who stayed at the ranch for a short while and broke hosses like a veteran while he tried to mend men's souls. He had been a deep one. He had fought like a wildcat – and it had taken Slim almost an hour to master him. The sky-pilot had taken a hell of a beating and Luella had been so sorry about it all that she threatened to run away with him – and almost did. Maybe she would've if Slim hadn't threatened to follow them with a shotgun – or maybe she just wanted to hear him say something like that. Would he ever kill a man for her he wondered. It was a chilling thought.

The last one had been Olly Blake, the dark, handsome younker who came from Texas five months ago. Olly was dead now. A month ago he had been found, shot in the back, by the waterhole in the glade. A fortnight after that Ep Simkins, a dour middle-aged man, had received the same treatment, shot from ambush up on the bluffs. Neither of them had had a chance. The pompous sheriff of Sorrowful Creek had done a lot of spouting and running around but he had not found out a thing. Neither had sorties from the ranch been any more successful.

Now, another fortnight after the death of Simkins, Shorty Mann had been shot at, but he had been luckier. Queer coincidence that new gink being there at the time. Maybe he had something to do with it. Or maybe the bushwhacker, thinking he was a Curly Bar 6 man, had meant to get him too. What was behind it? – was it the work of a band of rustlers trying to frighten cowhands away from the ranch so that they could make a haul? Or was there some deeper meaning?

No wonder the Old Man brooded more than ever of late and was cantankerous and savage. Slim Grady looked along to the head of the table, at the leonine grey head bent there, and suddenly felt a queer compassion – a surge of pity.

FOUR

Shorty looked up as the doc came in, the sheriff looming behind him.

' 'Bout time you got here,' he said. 'This damn' slug's borin' its way through to the other side – an' doin' a fandango while it's about it.'

Portly Doc Gruber cleared his throat with that little 'erump-rump' mannerism of his. He said: 'I waited for the sheriff. It took him longer than I thought it would. I knew a hard case like you wouldn't pass out for a little waiting anyway.'

Shorty ignored the flattery. He said: 'You didn't *hafta* bring the law with yuh.'

Sheriff Bart Gaylord stepped forward out of the late-afternoon gloom by the door. He said: 'You were bush-whacked, weren't you? The man who fetched the doc said you were. An' there's a stranger arrived, isn't there? Maybe he had something to do with it.'

'The stranger brought me in – he chased the bush-whacker. Maybe if he hadn't been there I'd've bin dead meat right now.' Shorty still was not easy in his own mind about the man who called himself Bert. But he would not have admitted that to the sheriff.

Gaylord stood beside the doctor, towering over him by at least six inches, his extreme leanness – some folks said he wore corsets – making him appear even taller. He thrust his head forward in that arrogant peering way of his and his General Custer goatee jutted from his chin. His lips were tight beneath his curled military moustache.

The long reddish-brown hair streaming over his shoulders was yet another part of the ensemble. He wore everything like they were stage-properties, but they were all real – as many a drunken stranger who had tried to yank the beard off, had found to his cost. Sheriff Gaylord could be mighty short with strangers, particularly drunken ones, and he had a liking for using his pistol-barrel like a whip.

He wore wrap-over coats and fancy cravats, and long, high-heeled riding-boots with fancy tops, and huge Mexican-type star rowels. He carried two guns, low-slung and placed butts inwards for a cross-arm draw. There were no real gunmen in Sorrowful Creek so he easily maintained his supremacy there.

'What did the bushwhacker look like?'

'How should I know? – I was knocked from my saddle like a bull had rammed me.'

'The stranger saw him, didn't he?'

'Not much of him I guess. He used a Winchester an' he was a long ways away.'

'Where is this stranger?'

Shorty jerked a thumb. 'In back.'

The portly doctor interposed himself hastily. 'Let's have a look at that shoulder.'

He sat on the edge of the bed and opened his little black bag. He cut the bandage away and made little clucking noises with his tongue.

The sheriff said: 'There ain't much light in here is there?'

'You like plenty o' light, don't you, Gaylord?' jeered Shorty.

'You're askin' for trouble.' The sheriff spun angrily like a ballet-dancer on his high heels. He crossed to the table in the middle of the bunkhouse and lit the lamp which stood there. The yellow light etched his straight form as he went back to the cot.

Shorty was lying on his back, his shoulder bare. The doctor took a bottle of whiskey out of his bag, poured some into a little silver cup and gave it to the cowboy.

'I've got to get that slug out, Shorty. I'll give you a whiff of chloroform if you want it.'

'Not on your life, doc. I like to see what's goin' on.'

Doc Gruber shrugged. He took a clean white cloth out of the bag, formed it into a pad and doused it with alcohol. Saying: 'This is gonna hurt,' he clapped it on to the wound.

Shorty's body tautened, his face, too; his lips like a trap – but no sound came from between them.

The doc gave him the cork out of the whiskey bottle. 'Bite on that,' he said. Shorty took it between tobacco stained teeth.'

Doc Gruber took out a long thin knife. 'Hold on to the sides o' the bunk,' he said, and he got to work.

Shorty felt like he had been bucked high in the air by a killer stallion and his body was being torn to pieces as he tossed and spun. When he hit the ground

41

there would be more blinding pain and that would be the end of it all. It seemed like there was a dark sky above him and somewhere amongst it a yellow sun. It was like that in the desert sometimes before the approach of a storm. He was hot too and everything was spinning and grinding and tearing and he felt he wanted to scream. But all the time he knew he must not. Like hell he mustn't!

Then there was final tearing agony and he thought he had hit at last. But things stopped spinning then, though they were a little hazy. The sun became static and he realized it was the lamp on the table. Then it was blocked out by a face, and Shorty said: 'What the hell are you grinning at?'

'I'm not grinning,' said Sheriff Bart Gaylord.

'There's the little crittur,' said Doe Gruber. He held the blood-stained slug in the palm of his left hand. He opened his mouth and shouted: 'Nolly!'

The cook stuck his huge black-jowled face through the kitchen door.

'Hot water here,' said Gruber.

'Comin' up, doc.' Nolly vanished.

A few seconds later he reappeared with a steaming kettle and a small enamel bowl.

'Bathe that wound,' said the doctor, 'while I get the bandages ready.'

Nolly set to. He had helped the little medico before. He seemed to notice the sheriff for the first time, or at least he acted that way.

'Howdy, John Law,' he said.

The sheriff grunted. His face, which might have been a little ratty without the beard and moustache, was a little redder than usual.

'Where's that stranger?' he said. 'I'd like to question him.'

'I've told yuh once,' said Shorty peevishly. 'He's in back. Hark at 'em whoopin' it up. Sounds like there's a fight in there or sump'n.'

'Call him, Nolly,' said the sheriff.

'I'm busy, call him yuhself.'

For a moment Gaylord looked like he would spring on the big man. Then he said huskily: 'Some day you folks'll really need the law. You'll need me an' a posse o' mine. Maybe you need 'em right now, though you don't realize it . . .'

He strode to the door of the mess-room and flung it open. The din subsided a little.

'Wal, if it ain't Two-gun Bill, the king o' the cowboys,' carolled a voice.

Then the three men in the bunkhouse heard the sheriff's voice and the din stopped altogether.

'I want the stranger who came in with Shorty.'

'Yuh don't hafta pull your irons on us, sheriff,' said a plaintiff voice. 'Cracker was on'y funnin'.'

'Where's the new man?'

'I'm the new man,' said a level voice.

'Come out here with me,' said the sheriff. Then he backed into the bunkhouse. His guns were out and Bert Johnson followed him.

'There warn't no call for a play like that,' said Nolly.

Just then the door flew open and in marched the Old Man with Slim Grady behind him.

The Old Man stopped dead, his face gone suddenly white. Then, his fists clenched and held out in front of him, he started forward once more.

'Boss,' said Slim, and caught hold of his arm.

The Old Man swung the arm back savagely, sending his young *segunda* reeling. The sheriff turned at the ranchowner's irate approach.

'Hold it,' he said.

Menaced by the levelled guns the Old Man stopped in his tracks.

'What's the meaning of this, you dressed-up hyena,' he said.

The words would have been funny had they not been spoken in such a thick rage-trembling voice.

The sheriff, when he spoke, sounded just as het-up. 'I came here in the execution of my duty and your men have done nothing else but try and make things as awkward as possible for me. Another man's been shot – a stranger has arrived. He's workin' for you – who is he? – where's he come from?'

'If I'd thought he'd got anythin' to do with the shootin' I wouldn't've set him on, would I?' The Old Man started forward again.

The sheriff jerked his guns. 'Get back. I've stood enough here. I aim to do my duty here whether you like it or not. I aim to ask this young man some questions.'

The sheriff stepped back a little so that everybody was before him and he could watch the door to the mess-room and the outer one too. The doctor and Nolly carried on with their ministrations of Shorty but they glanced at the armed man from time to time. The big cook's glance was murderous.

The Old Man stood with his head thrust forward like a buffalo getting ready to charge. His seamed face

44

was white, his walrus moustache seemed to bristle and there was something in his deep-set eyes that was more than mere temper.

Slim Grady stood behind him and a little to the right of him. The young ramrod, like all of them there apart from the truculent sheriff, was unarmed. He was tense like a coiled spring. He took a couple of long cat-like steps forward. He passed the Old Man.

'Back up I said,' the sheriff barked.

Slim stood still. 'Now what, fancy-pants?' he said. Bert Johnson was nearest to the sheriff. He had not moved and looked as phlegmatic as ever.

The sheriff jerked his head in that direction. 'Where'd yuh come from, son?'

'Oklahoma.'

'What part?'

'Muskogee.'

'Work on a ranch?'

'Yep.'

'What was the name of it?'

'Oxbow.'

'Just Oxbow, uh?'

'Oxbow Cattle Corporation, owned by a family called the Hallorans – about thirty of 'em all told, cousins an' all sorts.'

'I'll check on that.'

'You can check all you like. I left there a month ago an' I've been ridin' ever since. I been to lots o' places – see if you can check on them, too.'

'You trying to be funny?'

'Everybody else is makin' fun o' you, mister. I might as well too.'

Gaylord's lips opened in a snarl beneath his moustache. His right-hand gun twitched. For a moment everybody thought he was going to slash the young man across the face with it. But with an obvious effort he controlled himself. He said: 'I've a good mind to hold you for a suspect in these shootings.'

Nolly said suddenly: ' 'Bout time you had one, you've bin workin' on it long enough. How you gonna hold the feller?'

The Old Man's voice rasped harshly then. 'You ain't taking one of my men away from here on some trumpery charge.'

'Who's going to stop me?'

'You're in the wrong, sheriff, you might as well git,' said Nolly.

'Shut up, all of yuh,' said the Old Man. 'My patience is exhausted. Get off my spread, Gaylord. Go on, get going. If you come snoopin' around here again I'll have you horse-whipped.'

'I'm the law . . .'

'Get goin',' said the Old Man. He was trembling with rage. He began to move forward.

'Boss!' said Slim Grady.

'Get back,' said the sheriff. 'Back.' His guns were pointed directly at the Old Man's chest.

The door of the mess-room was suddenly flung open and Pat the Irishman came through. He stopped dead at the sight that met his eyes.

'What . . .'

The sheriff's eyes were deflected for a moment. Slim sprang between him and the Old Man. The sheriff fired. Slim dived forward and fell flat on his face.

The sheriff fired again and the shot knocked over the lamp.

'Johnson,' bawled Slim in an agonized voice. The room was plunged into darkness except for the shaft of light from the mess-room and that was blocked by the big Irishman. Pat gave a screech and started forward. The sheriff had moved into the shadows.

'Stay still every one of you,' he said. 'I'm goin'. Next time I come I'll bring a posse.'

The door banged then. 'Get him,' said the Old Man. His voice was hoarse with rage.

'Better let him go,' said Slim. 'I guess we've got enough trouble. He didn't hit me anyway.'

'Are you tellin' . . .'

'It's for the best, boss. After all he is the law.'

'Singin' small for a change, ain't yuh, Slim?'

'I'm thinkin' o' somep'n.' As Slim rose hoofbeats clattered away outside, faded into silence once more.

Slim crossed to the table. He picked up the broken lamp and lit up. The glass was smashed but the paraffin flame still illuminated most of the room.

He turned slowly towards Bert Johnson. 'You could've stopped him then,' he said. 'You was the nearest. He might've killed me. An' you didn't even move. What's the matter with you – yeller?'

'He's the law,' said Johnson imperturbably. 'Nobody was treatin' him right. He just wanted to ask me a few questions. I don't aim to get shot up by no lawman.'

'He wanted to take you in didn't he? He turned a gun on your boss. Who do you work for? What kind of a man are you?' The sheriff had gone but Slim had plenty more at which to rage. His lean body was beginning to tremble a little with temper, he could not keep his hands still.

He turned to the Old Man. 'This is a queer kind o' skunk we hired.'

Sometimes the ranch-owner seemed to delight in disagreeing with his volatile foreman. This time he merely vacillated.

'Mebbe,' he said. Then he looked at the newcomer. 'What's the matter with you, man? Why don't you stick up for yourself?'

'I can do that, suh.'

'Do it then, damn you!' snarled Slim.

He started forward and struck Johnson a ringing blow across the face with his open palm.

Johnson threw up his fists in a fighting stance. Slim backed away then came on again.

'Stop it!' The Old Man's voice sounded like a cracked bell.

Johnson dropped his hands. Slim stood away from him again. Everybody watched. Gawping faces looked over Pat's shoulder in the doorway of the mess-room. He held them back with a brawny arm resting on the door jamb.

The Old Man moved nearer to the two men. He looked into Johnson's face and something struggled deep down in those broody eyes, as if there was something about the yellow haired man he was trying to understand – even as if there was something he was trying to remember.

Doc Gruber said suddenly, softly: 'The young man was right. Nobody treated the sheriff properly. Shorty started on him as soon as he came in. What have you people got against the man?'

Shorty burst out: 'Two men got killed and he ain't done a thing about it. He wouldn't do no more to find out who bushwhacked me. I didn't want him meddling.'

'He's like a pesky musical comedy actor,' said Nolly the cook. 'He never should've been made a sheriff.'

'He's been trying,' said the portly doctor. 'I know that. You've got better men here than any of 'em in his posses, an' you haven't done any better. Whoever's doing all this shooting is keeping himself well hidden—'

'Nobody asked for your opinion,' said the Old Man.

'No, that's right, they didn't. I've done my job, I'll follow the sheriff.'

'Send me your bill.'

'I'll do that.' The door banged behind the little doctor.

The Old Man turned again on the two young men. 'So you want to fight, do you?' He raised his voice. 'Get plenty of lanterns. Bring 'em down to the big barn . . . Come on – both of yuh!'

FIVE

The big barn stood a little apart from the rest of the
out-buildings. It was used to store fodder for the horses
and the huge cleared space in its centre was a reposi-
tory for broken waggon parts and the like – as well as
an arena for the working off of surplus bile. Any man
who pulled a gun on a comrade at the Curly Bar 6 was
due for a quick kick-off. The Old Man favoured the
maulies – though, it was said, it hadn't always been
that way with him. Maybe that was why he was so all-
fired keen on them now.

The rubbish was quickly swept aside and the straw-
strewn clearing was ready for the two brawlers. They
stood apart and took off their upper clothing, standing
beneath the light and waiting for the word from the
Old Man.

'No holds barred,' he said. 'An' once you get goin' it's
a fight to the finish. On'y thing we draw the line at is
stranglin' an' gougin'.'

The two men nodded. Slim was the taller; his body
had a gleaming olive sheen except where it was sprinkled with fine black hairs. His shoulders were wide

and sloping, his chest deep-tapering down to a wash-board middle which would have delighted the eyes of a health and strength expert. He was rangy and supple and muscles wriggled like springs beneath his skin as he loosened himself up and scuffed his feet in the dry dust like a horse raring to go.

Bill, the stable lad, stood behind him, knowing he should not be there at all but seeking to ward off any reprimand by holding the foreman's clothes.

In the opposite corner stood Bert Johnson. He was more stolid, more stocky. His body was almost hairless, his chest square, his shoulders hunched. His legs were spread apart and his arms dangled. Yet, with that hunch of his shoulders and little forward thrust of his head, he seemed ready to spring forward any time.

Pat the Irishman stood behind him, the newcomer's clothes draped over his arm. Pat was beaming all over his red bovine face. Next to fighting himself there was nothing he liked better than watching others at it.

Gil Pendexter stood a little sullenly near him. Pat grinned at him and winked. Pendexter managed a sickly smile. His hand was wrapped in a soiled hand-kerchief, there was a red swelling on his jaw. He watched Pat warily. If the fight was a good one who knew whether the moody devil would get his blood up once more and strive to emulate the contestants.

It looked like being a good fight. The men were fairly evenly matched. Johnson had the advantage in weight but Slim probably had the longer reach. He was a seasoned fighter, too, and as fast and light-footed as a cat. He knew more fancy tricks than a gopher.

Everybody watched the Old Man. It was an irritating trait of his that, in affairs of this sort, he always took his time. It was almost as if he sat there and licked his lips in anticipation . . . How his deep-set eyes shone when he saw the blood too! For a moment he lost that brooding, tortured look.

Now he was sitting on a chair Nolly the cook had brought in for him. He was leaning forward a little, his big hands, fingers spread, resting on his thick knees. He looked slowly from one to the other of the contestants as if he was weighing them up. Then he said: 'All right, get goin'.'

Slim began to move forward on the balls of his feet. Johnson shuffled flat-footed, not so fast. He was barely away from his corner when Slim reached the centre of the ring. Then the young ramrod sprang. Johnson's fist went up into a fighting stance. His left shot out, stiff like an iron bar. It got in Slim's way. He pulled up short, ducked, Johnson's right came round and buffetted his shoulder. Wide-eyed, Slim spun. Johnson's left jabbed, straightened Slim up with a blow in the mouth, bringing the salty taste of blood. Then the right came again, flush on the jaw. Slim went flat on his back.

He jack-knifed and kicked out with his legs, expecting the new man to jump him. But Johnson merely circled and waited. As Slim rose warily there was surprise in his eyes and a little respect. Not because Johnson had not jumped him – maybe the man had been wise at that, for Slim was a real salty wrestler – but because Johnson was handier with his maulies and faster too, than the Curly Bar 6 champion had expected him to be.

Slim began to circle too. They followed each other

round like a couple of dogs. The tumult that greeted the first tumble had died. 'Get on with it, ye silly men,' growled Pat.

Slim's boots went 'slap-slap,' bringing little puffs of dust from the ground, as he moved in swiftly. His chin was tucked into his shoulders, his arms went like pistons. Johnson smothered them with suddenly crossed arms, the blows thudded on his forearms. Johnson swayed back on his heels. Thrown a little off balance, Slim lurched forward. Johnson's left shot out again, once more into the young ramrod's bruised mouth. Slim back-pedalled; Johnson's follow-up blow missed him entirely.

Slim spat blood into the dust. The crowd murmured. Johnson, his fists up in a correct rather awkward stance, waited again. A few in the crowd grumbled. This was too slow for them: why didn't the big feller follow up his advantage instead of prancing about like a fancy fighter in a tournament?

Slim did not move in again. He waited too.

'Get on with it!' yelled somebody.

Johnson began to move forward, flatfooted, his fists stuck up in front of his nose. Slim grinned with battered lips and leapt sideways suddenly like a playful kitten. Johnson turned to face him once more but he was not quick enough. Slim leapt in under his guard – wrapped his arms around his waist.

There was a grunt from Slim, a roar from the crowd, and Johnson was thrown. He hit the ground with a dull thud. Slim threw up his arms and leapt again like a man jumping lightheartedly into a pool. His knees came down hard on Johnson's stomach: Johnson's agonized gasp was clearly heard by all. Then the bigger man was using his knees and the crowd roared again as Slim was catapulted over his head.

Pat the Irishman jumped out of the way. 'Get him,' he roared.

But Johnson rose slowly, half-turning on his knees. He watched while Slim rose then he rose too. The two men faced each other once more. Slim seemed to take a deep breath. Then he rushed.

Johnson side-stepped and, as Slim lurched, hit him, in a buffetting round-arm blow, on one ear.

Slim staggered, twisting. Johnson's next blow missed him. He shook his head violently to drive off the bees which seemed to be buzzing around inside it. Johnson was moving in again, the correct fighter once more.

There were ringlets of blonde hair over his eyes. His face was set, his light-blue eyes fixed on his opponent. There was not a mark on his face but his broad, muscular light-skinned body was beginning to assume a mottled colour. Slim glared: there was something he did not understand about this man. Johnson showed no outward rancour. So far he had not lost his temper. But it seemed to the foreman that there was something very menacing about those queer eyes, like chips of blue ice in the lantern light. Maybe the man was taking this fight more seriously than he appeared to. More seriously than Slim was. To Slim it was just another fight: he had had hundreds of them. Maybe it was more than that to Johnson, maybe when he fought he hated a lot too, deep inside of him. To Slim it seemed there was something a little inhuman about him.

The crowd was grumbling again at the inactivity. Slim moved forward purposefully. Johnson watched him, sliding a bit, sideways. Slim bared his teeth and leapt once more. This time, however, he had changed his tactics. He went down suddenly, almost on his haunches, and struck low. Johnson doubled up as two terrific blows sank into his middle. Slim straightened out like an uncoiled spring and uppercutted him. Johnson's heels left the floor and he crashed on his back once more.

The crowd roared. 'Get him, Slim,' screamed Gil Pendexter.

He had not liked how the stranger had sat by and watched him get it from Pat. Any reasonable man would have interfered. This Johnson did not seem a reasonable man: he was a queer cuss all round.

Slim bent, grabbed Johnson's shoulders and hauled him to his feet, he held on with his left and drew back his right for a finishing blow.

'Your knee, Slim,' yelled somebody.

It was the old cowboy way of finishing off an opponent, a powerful jab under the jaw with a thrusting knee. A cruel way, more than one man had had his jaw broken by it.

But Slim did not use it this time. His fist thudded into Johnson's mouth. The man squirmed, slipped out of Slim's grasp; his face streaming blood.

The man was tough. Slim knew he could not grab him again. He stood away, waiting for him to get to his feet – then he rushed. Johnson adopted his fighting stance again; his set, bloodied face looked over his blood-stained fist. The face seemed to leer into Slim's

56

as the young ramrod struck and felt his blows parried once more. Then a right-hand jab in the chest sent Slim staggering away. Johnson was far from beaten. And he used his mitts like a professional! He shuffled forward after Slim, throwing blows right and left. Then they stood toe-to-toe in the middle and slugged. Slim's superior reach began to gain him an advantage. He fought Johnson off.

Johnson began to back-pedal, to guard himself once more. To feint, to bob and weave. Once more Slim became flummoxed by science and began to take punishment. He took blows again and again in the face and under the heart. His face, beneath the blood which mottled it, became white and drawn with pain. Johnson was like an inhuman fighting machine. Slim tried to cover up, to dodge, to retaliate. Always that half-crouching man was there, that seemingly awkward guard blocking his blows, the fists shooting out like pistons to cut his face to ribbons, bringing clutching pain to his heart.

Finally a terrible blow crashed on the side of his head. The lights, the towering bales of straw, the ceiling, the faces – all spun around him and he hit the floor. Things still swayed around him, like he was lying flat on his back on the saddle of a galloping horse.

Then the sensation stopped and he was looking at the roof of the barn, gradually getting it into focus, raising his pounding head and seeing Johnson still standing before him.

Slim gritted his teeth and began to rise. He got up on to one knee and everything spun around him once more. He could hear the men yelling encouragement.

Johnson was the shimmering shape in front of him: he braced himself then he rose and launched himself forward, all in one mighty effort. He felt wild exultation as his hand grasped the flesh of Johnson's heavy body. Then they crashed to the ground together.

Slim felt the body squirming beneath him. He hit out savagely, desperately. Then his arms were pinioned. The crowd roared as the two men rolled on the floor together. Their faces tossed garishly in the flickering light of the swinging hurricane lanterns. Their eyes shone, their mouths yammered. Things were livening up now. The Old Man leaned forward in his seat like an old dog crouched over a bone. He even growled deep in his throat, and his hollowed eyes shone.

Johnson was strong. He heaved Slim away from him and rose. Slim rose too. He had regained his strength. Johnson hit him on the temple, sending him staggering. Then he followed up, slowly, purposefully, a fighting machine once more.

Slim regained his balance and came forward to meet him, a little slower than usual, a little less sprightly. He was game to the last but he was fighting a losing battle against the inhuman man who carried himself like a professional mauler.

Johnson parried his blows again with childish ease and forced his own home. He almost seemed to be pulling his punches now, as if he took delight in cutting the young ramrod slowly to ribbons.

'Finish it!' yelled somebody.

The Old Man continued to lean forward in his seat like a graven image. He did not say a thing.

58

Slim was driven slowly around the arena by
Johnson's blows. From time to time he got one in
himself but there was no power behind them. He was
staggering, taking terrible punishment. But still he
remained on his feet and would not give in.

All heads turned as there was a cry from the direction of the door. Then Luella burst into the arena. Slim
was turning to look at her when Johnson's right fist
caught him on the side of the jaw. The smack of it was
like the distant sound of a rifle shot.

Slim went down flat, twitched and lay still. Johnson
backed away and dropped his hands. He was battered
too but he looked as unmoved as ever.

The girl stood as if transfixed.

'Luella,' barked her father. 'What are you doing
here?'

She paid him no heed. She ran forward towards
Slim. The young ramrod's powers of recovery were
remarkable. He was beginning to rise when she went
down beside him.

She put her arm around him and helped him up.
She looked at Johnson. Her dark eyes were unfath-
omable. He returned her look. There was nothing in his
face. Nothing at all.

'Are you all right, Slim?' she said.

'I'm all right.' He shook her hand away and stood
erect. He swayed a little but he stood away from her.
Despite the beating he had received he evidently did
not want a woman fussing him, he meant to stand on
his own two feet.

The Old Man rose. 'The party's over,' he said. 'You
got yourself whupped, Slim. Luella, you get out of here.'

The girl turned. It was as if she noticed her father for the first time.

'Luella – get out of here,' the Old Man repeated. 'This is man's business.'

Her eyes blazed. 'You encourage them in it,' she said. 'You love it don't you? Why don't you just let them shoot each other, it would be quicker.'

With that last cryptic remark she spun on her heels and flounced from the barn.

SIX

It was the day after the fight in the barn. Men were still talking about it. Things were quiet. Nobody had seen hide nor hair of the sheriff and nobody else had been shot. Things went on at the Curly Bar 6 as if nothing had ever happened to mar the even hard-working flow of ranch life.

It was Saturday and those of the men who had no special riding duties were on a half-day. Pay day wasn't till next week and most of them were getting a little short of cash so there was no slicking-up to go to town. That would come in the evening – for those lucky ones who still had enough lucre left to afford to go on a short spree.

It was a sunny afternoon and men were hunkered down against the bunkhouse wall smoking and yarning. Others were inside playing cards with the wounded Shorty. From the direction of the kitchen came the voice of Nolly singing 'The Cowboy's Lament' as he finished his chores. He sounded like a lovesick bull.

Another bunch of men were gathered at the corral

fence watching the antics of 'Firecracker,' the silver-grey stallion who nobody had yet succeeded in breaking.

They were climbing on the top rung of the fence, waiting till Firecracker made a wicked run at them and then jumping off with shouts of laughter. The stallion, one of the last wild horses of the territory, who had recently been caught, rolled his eyes wickedly and gnashed his teeth. He narrowly missed the seat of one cowboy's pants and his teeth took a chunk out of the fence. The cowboy started back as he thrust out his long neck like a striking snake and had another go.

The horse screamed with rage then began to run around the corral kicking up his back legs. He was boiling over with sheer murder. He made a full circle and came back to the area of the fence where the yelling cowhands stood. Then he changed his tactics, spinning suddenly and kicking backwards viciously. The cowhands scattered. The flying hoofs snapped a huge piece out of the middle rung of the fence. It spun through the air and struck one of the men in the face. With a cry of pain he went down, blood streaming from him.

The horse screamed again with a note of triumph. He bent his long neck and tried to get it through the gap in the fence. He could not make it, so he withdrew and pranced away again.

The wounded man was helped to his feet. There was a deep cut on his cheek. He dabbed at it with his handkerchief.

'I'll teach that crittur,' he said. 'Get me a saddle somebody.'

'You know what happened last time you rode him.'

'I can try again can't I? If he tries too many of his tricks I'll beat his durn' head off.'

While this had been going on Bert Johnson had been sitting on a disused waggon-shaft quietly smoking, a few yards away. Now he rose and strolled over to the group.

His face bore few signs of the mauling it had received the night before. It was as expressionless as ever – though perhaps not quite so smooth; and he didn't seem to see so good out of one eye.

'Did you see what that crittur did to me?' said the irate cowhand.

'Yeh, I saw it. He certainly got his own back.'

Another man approached with a saddle. 'Here yuh are, Coony.'

'Watch my smoke,' said Coony. He took the saddle, still dabbing his face with the other hand. 'Some of you help me to catch that durned hoss.'

The little bunch moved forward to the corral. Already others were coming from the direction of the bunkhouse to see what all the excitement was about.

One man uncoiled a lariat, waited till Firecracker quit his high jinks a little and then roped him. The stallion squawled and bucked and kicked out but, with four strong men at the other end of the rope, he was slowly pulled, fighting all the time, to the fence.

'That certainly is some hoss,' said Bert Johnson. It was the first bit of enthusiasm any of the men had seen in him.

Coony and another man climbed atop the fence and attempted to put the saddle on the furious beast.

Coony, who was still bleeding and dabbing, had only one hand in commission. He nearly fell over the fence under the slashing hoofs of the horse, and only the fact that one of the men behind grabbed his legs prevented his doing so.

'You'd better get that face fixed first.'

'It's quittin' now,' said the adamant Coony. 'Let me get at that crittur while my blood's still up. Gimme a hand here.'

The horse was being almost throttled by the tight rope and showed no more inclination to buck. While he was outwardly docile they managed to get the saddle on him and Coony forked it.

'Let him go,' he yelled.

The roper slackened the loop and jerked it away. The horse threw up his head and snorted. Coony raked him with his spurs, took off his wide-brimmed Stetson and beat the horse over the head with it.

The horse whirled and threw up his back legs. The cowhands scattered as splinters flew from the fence.

'Yippee!' yelled Coony and held on.

His face began to stream blood once more but he did not heed it.

Slim Grady came running across the yard. 'What's goin' on here?' he shouted. 'What's Coony think he's doin'. He'll get himself killed.'

Slim's face was a mean-looking sight – and his temper matched it. He came to an abrupt halt at the fence, his heels kicking up dust.

'What's happened here? Who did this?'

'The hoss.'

'What you been doin' to him?'

'Nothin', Slim.'

'They was hazin' him and he tried to get his own back,' said Bert Johnson. 'That's natural.'

Indignant glances were shot at him by the men. Why was he, of all people, kow-towing to Slim? This new fellow certainly had a knack of getting in folks' hair.

'Oh,' said Slim. He looked at Johnson without rancour. Then he turned his head and bawled: 'Coony! Bring that hoss back here.'

A couple of the men sniggered. Slim's irate command did sound rather funny – particularly as the horse was bringing Coony instead of the other way about.

'Watch yourself!' yelled one of the men.

Firecracker was galloping right for the fence. Coony was beating him with the Stetson, raking his hide with the spurs, striving to make him stop and buck – but with no effect.

A runaway horse like that one, who was liable to smash both himself and his rider before he stopped, is the bane of every bronc-buster. The men crowded to the fence and waved their hats and screamed at Firecracker in an attempt to drive him back.

'Jump, Coony!' yelled Slim.

The horse thundered on. The men backed away.

As Firecracker crashed headlong into the fence Coony jumped. He cleared the saddle but caught his feet on the topmost rung of the fence. He pitched head-first into the bunch, bringing two of them down with him.

Firecracker screamed. The men scattered as wood

flew in all directions. Coony and his two pards rolled on the ground and cursed. Some of the fence still held. The horse turned away more slowly. His gait was a little unsteady.

'Rope him before he recovers,' yelled Slim. 'Or he'll be over this fence in a jiffy.'

The lariat-expert threw his loop once more. He and two other men hauled on the rope and ran around the fence until Firecracker was drawn to the other side of the corral.

'Sam – Johnny, go to the barn an' get some wood an' stuff pronto,' said Slim. 'Get this mess fixed.'

As the two men ran to do his bidding he went on: 'Who started this shindig anyway?'

'That hoss started kickin' up like he was crazy—'

'They was hazin' him,' put in Bert Johnson. 'None of 'em know how to handle a high-spirited beast like that. They'll finish up by *really* drivin' him crazy. He wants riding an' he'll fight – but he don't want a pack of jackasses yellin' at him.'

Slim turned and looked at Johnson a little queerly – he was still finding it hard to figure the man and, although he bore no malice for the beating he had received, he still did not trust Johnson, still thought there was something mighty queer about him.

One of the men said hotly: 'Do you figure you could handle that hoss, mister?'

'I could try.'

'Yeh, mebbe you could,' put in Slim. 'I remember you telling me you'd like to try him sometime. I guess now's as good a time as any, uh?'

'Sure,' said Johnson. 'Jest let him simmer down first.'

66

'We'll do that,' said Slim, 'while you get your tackle.' An arrogant man himself, and one who did not mind flaunting the fact, he was irritated by this man's quiet assumption of superiority.

Johnson turned away. 'I'll get my stuff.'

'I can't figure that bozo,' said the first man who had spoken. 'Who is he Slim? – the Old Man set him on purty quickly.'

'As far as I know he's just what he says he is,' said Slim. 'He gave the sheriff some sharp answers.'

If the lean young ramrod entertained any suspicions about Johnson he kept them to himself. At the bottom of him he was still a little hazy. He disliked the man, but hesitated to show it and take advantage of his position. He was salty but he was not spiteful – and he did not want to give the men any cause to think him so. Nevertheless, he decided to watch the new gink very very closely.

One of the men the other side of the corral yelled, 'There's somebody comin' hell-for-leather across the mesa.'

'Sufferin' polecats,' said Slim. 'What's happened now? There ain't another one o' the men got hurt is there?'

He ran to join the two men who still held the snorting Firecracker at the end of their rope. The horse was cooling down.

The rider came down the slope at breakneck speed, dust billowing away from behind his horse. It was young Pete Locus. He was a mad-headed young cuss at the best of times. He was waving one arm above his head and yelling like an Indian. He drew up in another cloud of dust.

Slim scowled. 'What's eatin' you?'

'The sheriff's caught the bushwhacker,' said Pete excitedly. 'He's got him in jail right now.'

'Who is it?'

'I dunno. Some stranger. Little fat feller with whiskers. Sheriff an' a coupla depitties brought him in fust thing. As soon as I heard I rode back to tell yuh.'

'How do they know he's the bushwhacker?'

'They found him skulking up on the bluffs. Looked like he'd been up there some time, watching this place.'

'Hum,' said Slim. Then: 'Did yuh get what the Ol' Man sent yuh for?'

Pete's face crumpled childishly. 'Gosh, no! I forgot all about it.'

'Go get it. Quickly, before the Ol' Man spots you back here.'

'Sure, Slim.' Pete turned his horse's head . . . 'Slim! You comin' in?'

'Later I guess. I don't figure that bushwhacker is gonna escape once the sheriff's got him – Gaylord'll make sure o' that after all the trouble he's caused. Get goin', an' don't stick around too long.'

'*Adios*,' said Pete, and thundered off.

Slim turned to the two men. 'Don't go tellin' the boys right off,' he said. 'Keep it to yourselves for a bit.' He added sardonically: 'I don't want a panic.'

'All right, Slim,' said one.

'Hey,' said the other. 'Here's the new man with his saddle.'

'All right, let that hoss go.'

They threw off the loop and Firecracker began to circle

the corral, snorting and shaking his head in defiance.

'Let's get around there,' said Slim. The two men followed him.

Bert Johnson was ready and waiting while a couple of the men finished their task of repairing the fence. A bigger crowd had gathered to see Firecracker put the new fish through his paces.

The fence was completed and the horse was looped once more. He began to kick and buck.

'He's rarin' to go agin,' said Coony. 'Plenty much horse that, Johnson.'

The new man did not speak. He climbed to the top of the fence. He seemed oblivious of everybody but the horse. He began to talk to it, so softly that the men could not hear what he said.

After some manoeuvring, with a wary eye on those wicked teeth and hoofs, he managed to get the saddle on and the cinch tightened. The horse trembled as the man took his seat.

'Let him go,' said Johnson.

The loop was loosened and jerked away. The horse stayed put, still trembling.

'Looks like I gentled the crittur after all,' said Coony scornfully. 'You suttinly picked the best time to ride him, Johnson.'

But the would-be bronc-buster had spoken too soon. The horse came alive like the suddenly lighted firecracker which gave him his name. The whole smooth perfect body vibrated as he screamed. Then he reared up on his hind legs.

'He's going over!' yelled a man, almost hysterically. 'Jump, Johnson!'

His knees bowed tightly round the horse's flanks, the new man held on. A shrill whistle came from between his teeth. He did not use his Stetson, he just slapped the horse's neck with his hands. His Stetson fell from his head and spun in the dust.

A hissing murmur of relief came from the watchers as Firecracker came down on all fours. The jolt made his powerful body vibrate once more. Johnson's face was shot with pain as the shock travelled up his spine and felt like it was trying to blow the top of his head off. Then the sky spun around him as Firecracker began to buck.

That horse knew all the tricks – they just came natural to him. He sunfished, he turned himself into a hoop, he tried to snap his rider in mid-air, he spun: he did everything but a perfect cartwheel, and he came very near to that.

The man on his back was tossed and torn and buffet-ted. A few times daylight showed between his backside and the saddle. Were it a fancy rodeo he would have been disqualified. But it was no rodeo, and the yelling boys at the fence were not judges. Firecracker was no rodeo mount either: he was a mean, vicious back-breaking killer.

He came down from a high leap and Johnson sagged across his neck. But Firecracker gave him no respite: he was being tricky; he suddenly began to spin around in a circle, and Johnson had to make a frantic grab at the mane to prevent himself from falling sideways from the saddle.

The crowd applauded, but whether for the horse or the man was hard to define. To Johnson they were just a shimmering mass of whiteness that came into his orbit from time to time. The corral fence was just lines on a diffused backcloth. Then Firecracker changed his tactics once more and tried to reach the clouds in the sky. Earth, space, buildings, fences and men were a whirling kaleidoscope. Then there was the crashing, agonizing shock as the horse's four feet hit the ground once more and Johnson felt like his body was being torn to pieces.

His legs were not there any more, they were just parts of the throbbing horse, mere channels of burning agony.

Firecracker screamed and whirled and his neck snaked backwards. His teeth clicked in front of the cowboy's face. Johnson hit him across the neck with his fist.

The horse bucked again. Came down; bucked again; and again and again. The man on his back looked like a rag doll, glued there, being tossed from side to side, threatening to burst any moment and throw sawdust all over the place. The men yelled and above their voices the horse's scream rose once more.

Then the men became silent as from the ranch house the Old Man came hobbling. It was not often that he took any interest in what his men did in their spare time. What was up? Maybe he did not like Firecracker being ridden. Although it was not strictly his horse: the men had caught him themselves ... Still, a little item like that wouldn't worry the Old Man if he had his dander up.

Firecracker bucked and bucked – but he was beginning to lurch a little each time he came down. With one eye on the horse and rider and the other on their boss the men waited. The Old Man did not speak. They parted to let him through. He joined Slim at the rail. Slim saw the smouldering eyes looking at him and said: 'Afternoon, suh.'

The Old Man merely grunted. He leaned on the fence and watched the performance. The men became easier: they almost forgot his presence as they began to yell again.

Firecracker had begun to run. Round and round the corral, gathering speed all the time. And Johnson leaning forward over his neck, looking almost as if he was talking into the beast's ear.

Firecracker was getting closer to the fence all the time. 'Watch him, Johnson!' yelled Coony, fearful that the beast would try and pull the same trick on the new man as he had pulled on him.

Johnson was pulling the horse's neck on the right-hand, the side nearest to the fence, as he ran. He seemed to be talking urgently too, or maybe he was cursing.

'I never saw the guy flap his jaws so much since he got here,' said one man.

The Old Man, his shoulders hunched, leaned forward over the fence, his craggy, predatory face outthrust as he watched. No sound came from his set lips. Slim looked at him queerly. Often this moody old man made his young ramrod feel uncomfortable and rather creepy. There was something about Johnson, for all his blunt, healthy looks, which affected Slim the same way. Some similarity maybe about the eyes . . .

Slim's speculations deserted him as Firecracker

came in close. Slim backed away. The Old Man stood his ground – like a rock. The horse thundered on. Round and round, round and round.

At the opposite side of the corral from the bunch he suddenly veered away from the fence and began to race straight for the yelling men.

'Quiet,' said the Old Man suddenly.

It was as if somebody had suddenly fired a gun. The silence was absolute except for the drumming of hoofs on the hard sod, the panting of the horse; dust chittering and blowing into the men's faces.

Johnson was sitting upright in the saddle. His face was white and grimy, his blonde hair blew in the wind. He threw his weight sideways, holding on like a vice with his knees, leaning as far over as he dared without toppling from the saddle.

The men at the fence scattered. 'Boss,' said Slim. The Old Man did not heed him – or attempt to move. Slim stayed by his side and watched the awesome approach of the horse. He was coming at breakneck speed yet he did not seem to be getting nearer very fast. The corral seemed big, hellishly big.

Finally Slim realized that Firecracker was slowing up, veering a little. He saw Johnson's face once more. It was almost unrecognizable, so strained was the expression upon it.

Firecracker began to tack over like a ship hit by the wind. His eyes were rolling, his breath coming in gusty pants. Even from where he stood Slim could see the sweat standing out in great globules upon his hide. As he watched, Firecracker drew slowly to a halt. He stood still, trembling a little.

Johnson lurched forward over his neck. Slim took a lariat from one of the men and got through the fence.

'Be careful, Slim,' said the owner of the rope.

The ramrod went across the corral away from the horse as if he had not noticed his presence. Firecracker watched him out of the corner of his eye but made no movement. Slim began to move in slowly.

Johnson said softly: 'I don't think you'll need that rope.' He began to descend stiffly from the saddle. He seemed to be talking again, but even the ramrod could not hear what he said.

The short hairs at the back of Slim's neck began to prickle: he still did not trust that crittur. However, he wasn't going to let Johnson think that he was in any way scared. He coiled the lariat and tossed it to its owner on the other side of the fence.

Firecracker started a little at the sudden movement. 'Easy, boy,' said Johnson. Slim heard his words that time.

The blond-haired man let go of the horse and began to walk. As he got nearer to Slim he lurched. Slim caught hold of him.

Johnson shook him off. 'I'm all right,' he said. 'The hoss's all right now. He's broken good. I want a bridle. I've got to get back to him – he might get scared.'

'I'll get a bridle,' said Slim. He scowled as he went back to the fence. There was an ill-favoured galoot for you! When he looked back Johnson was returning, rather unsteadily, to the horse.

Slim got what he wanted and took it back to him. A few minutes later Johnson had Firecracker all slicked-up and ready for riding. He led him back to the bunch at the fence.

There were congratulatory murmurs. Only Pat, the big redheaded, freckle faced Irishman was loud in his praises. And he shut up when the Old Man spoke.

'That was good ridin', Johnson.'

'Thank you, suh.'

'You broke the horse – he's yours.' That Firecracker was not strictly his to give away did not seem to occur to the boss of the Curly Bar 6.

Johnson's reply was still more surprising. 'Thank you, suh, but I've already got a fine hoss. I guess he'd be jealous if I took another one – he's mighty mean when he's jealous.' He paused. Then he jerked his thumb and said: 'He's a grand horse. All the viciousness is worked out of him. He's as gentle as a baby. Maybe your daughter 'ud like to have him, suh.'

'Thank you, cowboy.' The voice came from the back of the crowd.

The ranks parted to let the girl through. She was dressed in her cowgirl costume, her long black hair tied back with a red ribbon. Her white teeth flashed in a smile.

The Old Man turned ponderously. 'Luella, what are you doin' here? I told you to keep away.'

'I watched the ride from my window,' said the girl. She went closer to the Old Man, linked her arm in his. 'I may have the horse, mayn't I, Dad? – he's such a beautiful beast.'

The Old Man looked down at her. Then he looked at Johnson who stood silently by, his white, weary dirt-streaked face as expressionless as ever. Something flickered in the depths of the Old Man's eyes: it was not pleasant. He looked at the girl again and grunted. It seemed he could not refuse. Whether or not, the girl took the grunt for 'Yes'. She let go of him and ran to the fence. She reached over and stroked the horse's glossy neck. He turned to look at her and there was no rage in his eyes now. The girl turned and looked at Johnson.

'Thank you, cowboy,' she said again.

'You're welcome, miss,' he replied. He spun on his heels and limped off towards the bunkhouse. Pat the Irishman ran after him, caught up with him and fell into step with him.

A man in the crowd said softly: 'There's a man who's good an' knows it.'

'He's too damned good,' said his neighbour.

His words summed-up the attitude of most of the boys towards Johnson. Only Pat seemed to have really cottoned on to him. Despite the dissimilarity of their tempers there was something very much alike in the two men.

SEVEN

After their early evening meal a bunch of the boys, with Slim at their head, rode into Sorrowful Creek to have a look at this bushwhacking fish the town's illustrious sheriff had succeeded in netting.

Among the bunch were Johnson, Pat and Gil Pendexter. As soon as they got in town the foreman left them and made for the sheriff's office. The rest went into the Billy Boy saloon. They were greeted with much whooping and insulting by a bunch of boys who were playing poker in the corner.

'They come from the Triangle Plus Ranch,' Pat told Johnson. 'Their land adjoins ours – matter of twelve miles away. The Ol' Man an' Ep Browning, who owns the Triangle Plus, ain't spoken to each other f'r years. The Ol' Man's got the biggest holdings I guess – but ol' Ep comes mighty close – got some good beef too . . . What ye havin', Bert?'

'Straight rye,' said Johnson.

The Curly Bar 6 men made a crush at the bar. Gil Pendexter pushed his way between Johnson and Pat.

'Hallo, runt,' said the latter. 'What'll you have?'

Gil still showed signs of the rough handling he had received from the big fellow the night before.

He mumbled something and withdrew. Pat's laugh boomed out. 'Suit y'self,' he said. He turned to Johnson. 'I'd've bought the man a couple of drinks,' he said. 'I don't bear anybody malice y'know. It's me temper – it'll be the death of me yet.'

'There's many a true word spoken in jest,' quoted a Triangle Plus man behind him. This latter had forsaken his poker and together with most of his pards, was pushing to the bar with the Curly Bar 6 men.

'Begob, man,' boomed Pat. 'Oi'll live to be a hundred an' twenty.'

At times his brogue was more pronounced than others. This was one of those times. Pat was in good humour. He began to exchange good-natured chaff with the Triangle Plus men. He introduced them to his friend, Bert, 'the hottest li'l bronc-buster they'd ever seen.' Johnson acknowledged their greeting but did not join in their badinage. He seemed to be imbibing liquor pretty fast and rather morosely, like a man accustomed to drinking by himself.

Pat was telling his friends an Irish joke when Slim entered the saloon. Immediately attention was turned to the young ramrod. Pat's joke petered out and he joined the ranks of the questioners. Again Johnson did not take part in the general mêlée but he was seen to start and come away from the bar as Slim described the sheriff's prisoner.

He was a little tubby man with luxurious black whiskers and a bald patch. Slim had seen him. He seemed a harmless sort of cuss. He kept protesting his innocence, saying he'd come to that part of the country looking for a job and was just investigating the lay of the land when Gaylord and his men jumped him. He carried a Winchester and a Colt forty-five . . . still, so did hundreds of other cowhands, many of them right here in the saloon this very minute.

'Sure,' said somebody else.

'Do you think he's the bushwhacker, Slim?' asked another.

'It's possible. People ain't always what they seem. The sheriff seems to think he's guilty.'

'Has he got any proof?'

'He talks like he has – but he won't say what it is.'

'What's the bushwhacker call hisself?'

'Steve Lasare. He's a Texan.'

Johnson spoke then. 'He's my pard. He said he'd catch up with me here. He's no more a bushwhacker than I am.'

His sudden spurt of anger died as quick as it was born. Slim, irritated by his sudden outburst, said: 'We don't know a lot about you, mister.'

Johnson either did not hear him or was indifferent to what he said. He brushed past the ramrod and made for the door. Pat followed him.

At the door Johnson turned. 'Stay here,' he said to the Irishman.

A little disgruntled, Pat turned to the bar, and knocked back a glass of rye with an air of martyrdom.

One of the Triangle Plus men said, 'Wal, can you beat that? That new fish o' yours is suttinly a queer one, Slim.'

Pat thrust his way to the man and stuck his huge

freckled visage in front of him. 'Bert don't say much,' he said. 'But he ain't done you any harm. Shut your face will yuh?'

'Yeh, sure, Pat,' said the man hastily. 'I didn't know he was a pard of yourn.'

'Wal, he is,' growled Pat. His little eyes had grown choleric. He looked around him with disfavour. 'Lot o' cacklin' jackasses,' he said. 'Would any two of yez like to give me a couple of rounds with the fisticuffs?'

Everybody there had heard the naïve challenge before. Also they had seen what happened to men who were foolhardy enough to accept it. Nobody said anything for a bit. It was Slim Grady who broke the silence. He was probably the only one who dared.

'Simmer down, Pat,' he said. 'Come on an' have a drink all nice an' peaceful, an' wait for Johnson to come back.'

Pat turned and glared at the foreman. His huge hands opened and closed. The crowd held their breath.

Then Pat suddenly began to laugh. 'All right, Slim me boy,' he spluttered.

He put one arm around Slim's shoulders and the other around that of Gil Pendexter, who happened to be nearest. Pendexter wisely left it there. He was not taking any more chances with the unpredictable Irishman. Not while Pat had a hand on him anyway.

Sheriff Bart Gaylord took his feet off the desk as his door was rapped. His deputy, a squint-eyed man called George, stopped cleaning a shotgun and with a ferocious look on his simple face levelled it at the door.

'See who it is, you fool,' said the sheriff.

George rose, left the shotgun and crossed to the door. Gaylord dropped his hand to the butt of his gun.

George opened the door. Somebody said something. George said, 'Yeh, he's here. You got an appointment, mister?'

Then the door was flung wider and George went backwards. He finished up in a sitting position against the sheriff's desk and Bert Johnson strode into the office and closed the door behind him. He turned to look into the muzzle of the sheriff's Colt.

'That isn't the way to enter an establishment of the law.'

Johnson stood straddle-legged in front of the desk. 'You've got a friend o' mine in your cells,' he said. 'A man named Steve Lasare who never hurt a fly, let alone shoot anybody in the back. He worked with me at the Hallorans' Oxbow. He left with me. He stopped off at Tulsa to see his family – then he said he'd catch me up. He must've bin lookin' for me when you jumped him.'

'Coming in here raving like that isn't what I expected from you, young fellow,' said Gaylord. His gun remained steady. 'How do you know the man in the cells is your friend?'

'I've heard what he looks like an' I've heard his name. There ain't but one Steve Lasare who looks iike that.'

'And he was looking for you?'

'He was.'

'How did he know where you'd be? I thought you were a stranger here – just a saddle-tramp seeking work.'

'I was. But I told Steve which part of the country I was headin' for. I guess he'd ask around as he went along. I took my time an' I stopped plenty places.'

'The man didn't tell us he was looking for you. He didn't mention any names at all.'

'Wouldn't've been much use would it? He didn't know whether I was here or not.'

Gaylord rose and stretched himself languidly, his gun still pointed at the young man's chest.

'Take his gun, George,' he said.

George, on his feet once more, obeyed with alacrity. The glance he shot at the young man was murderous.

'Give me the gun, George,' said Gaylord.

He took it with his left hand and tucked it into his belt. He smiled at Johnson. Standing there with his moustache and flowing brown hair he looked a fine figure of a man; but Johnson was not impressed. He said:

'What's the game, *Mister* Sheriff?'

'Get over there, George,' said Gaylord. 'Cover him.'

George backed over to his corner and picked up his shotgun and levelled it at Johnson. Gaylord said: 'George has taken a dislike to you. If you make any funny moves he'll probably shoot you in the belly. Have you ever had a load of buckshot in the belly, young fellow? No, I don't expect you have. Very unpleasant I imagine; very unpleasant indeed.'

'You talk too much,' said Johnson.

Gaylord smiled at him and turned away. He might have been acting a part in a play. He unlocked the door to the right of his desk. As he did so he took a bunch of keys from somewhere beneath his fancy vest.

82

He disappeared from view as his feet echoed on the stone floor of the passage. The two men in the office heard his voice say loudly: 'Do you know a man called Bert Johnson?'

The reply was inaudible, a mere mumble.

There was a rattle of keys, the creaking of an opening door, the clang of it as it closed. Then the footsteps started up again, redoubled, coming back.

A little tubby man with a black curly moustache came into the office and stopped dead, blinking at Johnson. The sheriff, smiling behind him, had a gun in his back.

Johnson said: 'Howdy, Steve! Fine pickle you got yurself intuh. Gettin' intuh the clutches o' the law as soon as you land in the territory.'

'Uh, howdy – Bert,' said the little man. 'I've been lookin' all over for yuh. I thought I'd come to the wrong place again. I was up on the bluffs. I could see a couple of biggish clusters of ranch huildings.'

'I guess the one 'ud belong to the Triangle Plus,' said Johnson half to himself.

'I was hopin' to see somebody, to ask, maybe get a line on yuh. I sat up there restin' a while an' smokin'. Then this big fancy galoot an' his boys jumped me. They say I've bin livin' up there an' shootin' at people. What's goin' on. . . ?'

'Steve,' said Johnson. 'Have you told the sheriff where you came from an' everythin'?'

'I ain't told the big skunk nuthin'. I don't like bein' pushed around.'

'Tell him then. Go on, tell him. Tell him where we worked together an' all the rest of it.'

83

'All right – if you say so.'

'Wait a minute,' said Gaylord. He was not smiling now. 'A minute of two ago back there in the cells you told me you'd never heard of a man called Bert Johnson.'

Steve Lasare looked at him scornfully. 'I wasn't intendin' to tell you nuthin' atall. Not a durn thing. Anyway, I didn't want to drag Bert intuh anythin'.'

'Steve's like that,' said Johnson. 'Kinda bullheaded . . .'

'I'll talk if you say so, Bert,' said Lasare.

He told the sheriff of how he and Johnson left the Oxbow Ranch together, how they planned to seek a change of air and new jobs in this neck of the woods, of how Lasare dropped off at Tulsa to visit his brother and Johnson carried on.

'You see,' said the Curly Bar 6 man. 'Just like I told you. Why should Steve want to shoot anybody here? You just pulled him in to save your face because you figured he was a saddle-tramp with no friends an' maybe you could pin these killings on him. You haven't an atom of proof.'

Sheriff Gaylord smiled beneath his moustache. It was not a pleasant smile. He said: 'I've got proof all right.'

'I don't believe it. Show it to me.'

'Who do you think you are?' said Gaylord silkily. 'I shan't show you a damned thing. You'll see it at this man's trial the same as everybody else . . .' He turned on Lasare. 'Get back into the cells. Go on, move.'

'I don't know what your game is, Gaylord—' began Johnson.

'No game, my friend. You be careful or I'll clap you in the cells along with your so-called friend.'

'Take it easy, Bert,' said Lasare. 'Don't worry, this big fancy-man ain't got nuthin' on me.'

He winced as Gaylord jabbed him viciously in the back with the barrel of his Colt. Johnson started forward. George gestured with his shotgun and looked savage. The two men went down the passage. The cell-door clanged and Gaylord returned alone. He said: 'You'd better get goin', young fellow.'

'Give me my gun.'

'Oh, no.' Gaylord smiled. 'I'll tell you what I'll do. You ask your foreman, Slim Grady, to come and see me an' I'll give it to him.'

Johnson turned on his heels and left the office. As he closed the door he could hear the sheriff and his deputy laughing behind him.

He went back to the saloon. Pat was the first to greet him.

Johnson said: 'He's my friend all right. The sheriff's holdin' him.'

'Where's your gun?'

'The sheriff took it away from me.'

'Took it away from you?' Pat's voice was a little incredulous. Somebody in the crowd sniggered.

'You didn't try to bust your pard outa jail all on yuh lonesome did yuh, Johnson?' said one of the Curly Bar 6 men.

Johnson shook his head. His vocal chords seemed to have dried up again.

Slim said suddenly: 'No tinpot lawman's gonna take a gun off one o' my men.' He made for the door.

Johnson: 'There's no need for anybody to interfere.'

Slim half turned. He said: 'There's nothin' personal about this. Nobody does tricks like that on Curly Bar 6 folks that's all, no matter who they are. If the Ol' Man heard o' this he'd have a fit . . . Stay here, all of yuh,' he added brusquely. The batwings swung to behind him.

'Slim'll git that gun awlright, Johnson,' said one of the men. 'He ain't scairt o' no tinpot sheriff.'

Johnson said nothing. He stood beside Pat at the bar and tipped back more rye. The big Irishman was silent too. He kept looking at his companion as if he could not quite figure him out.

A short time passed. One of the men started to play the piano, another to sing. Then the batwings swung again and Slim reappeared.

He had an extra gun in his belt. He took it out and handed it to Johnson.

'There y'are, pardner,' he said.

Only Johnson, as he took the gun and sheathed it, saw the mocking light in the young ramrod's eyes.

EIGHT

The new man was up early the following morning. It was barely dawn and he was not due to go riding until seven. He wore a pair of flat Indian moccasins as he left the bunkhouse. He closed the door quietly behind him. He lit a cigarette and then began to walk slowly around the ranch-buildings. The corral was silent. Firecracker was no longer there. Johnson went on past the ranch house.

The pearly half-light brought lines and shadows to Johnson's smooth face. He looked very thoughtful as he walked and smoked. He was oblivious of the beauty and magic of the Western dawn, the delicate slowly-changing colours in the sky, the light rippling over the grass-lands, the faint blue haze on the horizon, a pink glow in the centre of it which proclaimed that already the sun was waiting to break through.

He wandered away from the ranch-buildings out on to the gently waving grass which lapped damply around his ankles. He was a little figure in a limitless void.

As the morning came he turned about and retraced

his steps. He saw figures coming out of the bunkhouse and going to the pumps around the back. He heard Nolly singing. He passed the ranch house; most of its windows still had curtains drawn across them, it looked a little chill and forbidding. He was passing the small stable which was attached to the house when a soft voice called his name.

He started and turned his head. Luella stood in the stable doorway and smiled and beckoned him. He looked around him and then he went over to her.

He was almost at the door when she vanished into the gloom of the stables. 'Come in here, Mr Johnson,' she called.

He went through the door and then paused, blinking as he looked around him in the soft gloom which smelled pleasantly of horses and hay and another smell; the scent a woman used. She stood in the end stall with her hand on Firecracker's neck.

'I want to thank you again for letting me have him, Mr Johnson,' she said. 'He's a beauty. We're great friends already. Look.' She put her hand into the front pocket of her riding breeches and brought forth a lump of sugar.

Firecracker took it daintily from her hand. She gave a ripple of laughter and looked up. Her eyes shone a little in the gloom and her hair was like black smoke. 'Come and see if he'll take it from you,' she said.

Johnson had not said anything at all. He covered the space between him and the girl in four long strides. She held out her hand and he took the sugar from it. He offered it to the horse between thumb and forefinger.

'Oh,' said Luella. 'Be careful.'

Firecracker stretched his long neck. He nudged Johnson's hand with his nuzzle then gently took the sugar. The man patted his nose. The horse finished crunching the sugar and nudged the man's shoulder. The girl said: 'You've got a way with horses, haven't you?'

Johnson turned and looked at her. 'I suppose I have, miss,' he said.

'Don't keep calling me miss,' she said. 'The name's Luella – as long as Dad doesn't hear you. Your name is Bert, isn't it?'

'Yes.'

'We've never had a cowboy named Bert here before.' The girl moved closer and looked up into the man's face. There was a little mocking light in her eyes, a half-smile on her lips. Johnson seemed born to be mocked. He was a big handsome lummox. Obviously Luella wanted to know whether he was as good with women as he was with horses.

'I want to thank you again for giving me Firecracker, Bert,' she said. It was almost as if she was on her tiptoes now. Her body was taut; she was high-breasted; lithe, beautiful.

She rested her hand on his arm. 'Thank you,' she whispered.

'He was yours all along, Luella,' said Johnson. 'He could not possibly be anybody else's.'

The girl's body came close to his and he put his arms around her. Her hands travelled caressingly up to his shoulders and then went around his neck. They drew apart as footsteps thudded behind them. Slim was coming into the stable. His lean dark face was white with passion, his eyes blazed. He flung a blow at Johnson. The yellow-haired man blocked it. But another one followed. Johnson was driven backwards by the mad fury of the attack. He struck blows in return but Slim did not seem to notice them.

A haymaker caught Johnson on the side of the jaw. His feet went from under him. As he fell his head hit the top of Firecracker's stall with a sickening thud. He sprawled in the straw at the horse's feet and lay still.

'Slim!' cried Luella. 'You've killed him.'

Slim went down on his knees. 'Naw, he's just stunned.' He rose again, swung round on her with such fury that she shrunk away from him.

'I was just thanking him, Slim, for giving me the horse.'

'The horse wasn't his to give in the first place. Still, it was a good excuse for you to set your cap at him wasn't it?' He growled deep in his throat and raised his hand. Then he let it fall. 'Bah, you're not worth it.'

'You brute,' she said. 'You filthy beast. You don't care whether you've killed that man or not, and now you want to strike me.'

'He's just stunned I tell you. Anyway, I owe him that . . . Maybe you'd like to stroke his head when he comes round.' There was pain in his eyes. He turned away from her.

'Slim,' she said. She followed him to the door.

He turned and grabbed hold of her suddenly. She shrank from the menace in his eyes but he held her close, glaring down into her face.

'I'll kill the next man I catch you with,' he said. 'Do

you understand? – no matter who he is I'll kill him. I know that, in most cases, you're as much to blame as any of them. I try to tell myself that you're not, but I know it ain't true. If I killed anybody you'd be as much to blame as me . . . God, I wish I didn't feel this way about you. The way you act is enough to drive a man crazy.'

He let her go, strode away from her. She stood uncertainly; she was trembling a little. He picked up the firebucket from beside the door and went back into the stable with it.

Over his shoulder he snarled, 'Get back into the house. Go on, get back into the house.'

Luella looked at him fearfully. He had never spoken to her like that before. She turned and ran to the house. On the veranda she stopped and looked back.. Slim was nowhere to be seen.

'Luella!' her father's voice thundered. 'Where in tarnation have you been?'

Johnson was coming round when the icy water hit him. He spluttered and sat up, rubbing his eyes, shaking himself like a huge dog.

Slim stood back and watched with ghoulish enjoyment. He swung the bucket back and forth in his hand, missing Johnson's face by an hairsbreadth. Firecracker looked on with a rolling speculative eye.

Dirty water ran down Johnson's face. He combed it out of his hair. He looked up at Slim. The lean ramrod said: 'That was my girl you were makin' love to.'

'Oh,' said Johnson a little foolishly.

'Yeh,' said Slim. 'We're engaged to be married.'

91

'I didn't know,' said Johnson. If other words trembled on his tongue he left them unspoken.

Slim said: 'I told her I'd kill the next man I saw her with.' There was no mistaking the menacing challenge in his voice.

'So,' said Johnson. Nothing more. He rose.

Slim said: 'You've whupped me once. But I ain't afeard to try again.'

'That'd be kinda silly,' said Johnson. He passed Slim and went out into the morning sunshine. The foreman shrugged, tossed the bucket into the corner and followed him. Firecracker watched him go then suddenly neighed loudly. It was almost as if he was laughing.

Slim almost jumped out of his skin. 'Durned crittur,' he said. 'I wish we'd never caught him.'

When he got outside Johnson was approaching the bunkhouse and did not look back.

NINE

Big Pat was chosen to show Johnson the ropes. The two men rode out to comb the brush for strays. It was the morning after the new man's second shindig with Slim. Nobody else knew about that.

Pat and Johnson plunged into the blue haze which encompassed the brush and lay in the hollows of the foothills. Pat was a good workman. Once on the job his volubility seemed to leave him. Or maybe he was still a little puzzled by his companion. Johnson was as taciturn as ever.

The sun came up and they had already driven three bawling mavericks from the prickly shrubs and coarse plaited grass.

'Ain't bin nobody out here in quite a while,' said Pat. 'The Ol' Man's slipping. He ain't the ol' tyrant he used to be.'

'If he ain't what he useter be he must've been a proper ring-tailed bobcat when he was in his prime,' said Johnson.

'He useter drive his men like dogs. Now he leaves most o' the runnin' o' the ranch to Slim. Slim's an ornery young cuss at times – but he's all right.'

'I've got nothin' agin Slim,' said Johnson shortly.

Pat changed the subject. 'There's a nasty little quagmire up ahead. More'n one poor little critter's finished up there. We'll go an' have a looksee.' He led the way.

They heard the frenzied bawling of a calf before they reached the spot. 'Looks like we're jest in time,' said Pat and spurred his horse forward. Johnson heard him cursing as his horse tore its way through the thick scrub. He was more careful with Blackie and the fleet, intelligent beast got along with as little hardship as possible to himself.

The soft ground was sucking at the horse's feet as he stepped daintily in the wake of Pat's mount. Then he halted behind him. The bawling calf was stuck fast almost in the centre of the small area of swamp-land.

Pat had uncoiled his lariat and was swinging the loop gently. His head was on one side as he calculated the distance. Then he tossed the rope and the loop fell gently over the beast's head.

Pat looped the free end over his saddle-pommel.

'Back,' he said. 'Back.'

Snorting, the horse backed; the calf bawled louder in fear as the rope tightened around his neck. The mud sucked audibly.

'We'll get the little critter out if we don't choke him fust,' said Pat.

Johnson urged Blackie to the side of the Irishman's horse. He took the dangling end of the lariat in his hand. He said, 'Mebbe if we pull this way, Pat . . . We

94

ain't so likely to have him over on his side and get him under again.' He eased Blackie over gently. Pat's horse followed.

The area of swampland was at the base of small foothills. Now the sun came through a cleft in the hills and spotlighted the little drama. Struggling as if he would rather stay where he was than be hauled out in that fashion, the calf was being drawn gradually nearer to the men and horses.

Johnson's plan was effective: the little beast was drawn forward in a straight line, leaving a scummy wake behind him. The mud lapped and sucked at his rump, very reluctant to let him go.

'Up, ye little spalpeen,' said Pat.

Johnson dismounted and, walking delicately, got as near as he could to the struggling beast. The high heels of his riding boots sank into the mud. He felt the power of it pulling at him. He spied something white and shiny a few yards away, the sun suddenly catching it. It was the bleached skull of a steer. The swamp was avid for other victims.

'Careful, Bert,' said Pat.

'Mebbe I can get near enough to get the rope under him . . .'

'Don't take any chances. Hell—'

Pat stopped talking. Then he made a queer choking sound. The flat echoes of a rifle shot rolled down from the hills and Johnson drew his gun. He turned.

There was a look of childish surprise on the Irishman's face. Then it crumpled in agony. He pitched forward and as he did so his startled horse lurched and its front legs sank into the oozy slime. Pat toppled from

95

the saddle and hit the mud belly downwards. It sucked at him greedily.

Johnson backed, his eyes raking the hills, his gun ready. He saw nothing. He reached Pat's side. He sheathed the gun. He bent and grabbed Pat beneath the armpits. He knew instinctively by the weight of him, the leaden dragging as his feet left the mud, that the Irishman was dead. Something buzzed past Johnson's head. He let Pat go as the rifle cracked again. He floundered, fell to his knees. Up in the rocks on the slopes of the hills something glinted. Johnson fired. He turned and vaulted into Blackie's saddle. He urged the horse along the side of the swamp to cover beneath an overhanging bluff. Another slug passed behind him. Then he was in cover. He slid from Blackie's back and with a smack on his rump urged him gently into the shadows.

Johnson looked towards the swamp. Pat's body was slowly sinking, sinking. His horse stood curiously by. The usually phlegmatic Johnson cursed slowly, softly, and with strained bitterness. Then he turned away, flattened himself against the bluff and began to work his way along the rock-face.

He reached the corner. He took off his Stetson and, holding it by the brim, pushed it cautiously around the corner. A slug ricocheted from the rock just above it. The echoes were awakened once more.

Johnson withdrew the hat. He retraced his steps along the rock wall, passed his horse. The rock-face was sloping there. He looked up. There was very little foothold. He stuck his toes into the rock and began to climb. He slipped back, one hand streaming with blood.

The bushwhacker must have heard the sound. He fired and the bullet kicked up the dust a few yards away from Blackie.

Johnson stood panting. The body of Pat was sinking further beneath the ooze. Johnson went back, further along the base of the sloping rock; he was moving further away from his quarry. Finally he halted and began to climb again.

Now the sun was growing more powerful. It beat upon the rock-face and was reflected back upon his face so that his eyes began to water. He kept his head low and felt for hand-holds as he climbed. Suddenly he realized that he was almost at the top. He stopped, panting.

After a moment he reached up and curled his hand over the top, and began to haul himself up. He got his head over, and looked around for his quarry. He saw what looked like a man's elbow, showing in a cluster of rocks above him. He realized he was a sitting duck himself. He must get into cover before he attempted to stalk his man or draw him out. A lone round boulder a few yards in front of him was his nearest and safest objective. He rose to his knees and drew his gun.

In a stooping position, he began to move towards his objective. He watched the thing between the rocks: was it a man's elbow or was he imagining things? The bush-whacker might have a bead on him right now from some other direction. The thought was chilling. He looked around him. It was then the thing he had been watching moved. Sunshine glinted on metal.

Johnson threw himself sideways. A slug whistled past him. The bark of the rifle was a flat vicious sound.

The sky spun above Johnson as he lost his balance. He fell on top of the slope and began to roll. He had a confused glimpse of the man up above him, standing tall and still, the glint of the rifle in his hands. Then the rifle barked again and he was rolling. A slug kicked the dust from the rock before his face. Then the world was spinning and he was falling and clawing. He hit the ground with a bump that jarred every bruised bone and muscle in his body. He was dazed. One thing he realized, with sudden fear, was that he had lost his gun in the fall. He sat up and looked upwards. He thought he heard a sound up there.

If the bushwhacker was coming out of hiding to finish him off he had a good chance of succeeding in his aim. Johnson felt defenceless and a little panicky. He wondered what his pards back at the Curly Bar 6 would think of him if they could see him now.

The body of Pat was buried to its shoulders in the mud. There was no chance of getting the Irishman's gun.

Johnson had left his own rifle back in the bunkhouse. A man did not think he would need such a thing when hunting strays. But the yellow-haired man thought he remembered that the Irishman had carried his Winchester in the boot beside the saddle. If he could reach that horse . . .

He made his decision. He rose and began to run. He had almost reached the horse when he heard boot-heels above him. He flung himself forward in one last desperate bid. He heard the smack of a bullet hitting flesh. The horse's scream drowned the sound of the shot. Then the horse fell, missing Johnson by a hairsbreadth. It landed beside him, twitched once, and lay still.

Johnson rolled into the cover of its inert body. He looked above him. He could see nothing. Evidently the bushwhacker was not keen on showing himself.

Johnson felt an overwhelming sense of relief when he saw that his late pard's Winchester was still intact in the boot. He reached upwards and pulled it free. He lay in the cover of the dead horse and waited.

He cursed softly when he heard the sound of hoof-beats on the hard rock. Up near the spot where the first shots came from he caught a glimpse of the crown of the man's hat. He raised his rifle. He lowered it again as the hat disappeared. The man was riding down the other side of the slope. As Johnson rose stiffly the hoofbeats were already fading. He knew that to follow the man directly he would have to climb over the hill. There was no chance of overtaking him.

He looked around for the calf which, after the shooting of Pat, had extricated itself and ambled off. He saw it in the brush a few yards away. It had gotten itself stuck once more. It began to bawl and thresh as he ran across to it. Pat's lariat still streamed behind it.

Johnson pulled the creature out of the brush and got the rope free. He ran to the edge of the quagmire. The shoulders of the body were almost submerged. Johnson was in up to his ankles. He got his hand into the ooze and found Pat's armpits. He hauled him higher and got the rope over the shoulders and under the armpits. Playing out the rope he backed gingerly, reached comparatively firm land, and whistled Blackie. When the horse came he fastened the end of the rope to the pommel and climbed up into the saddle.

'Pull, boy,' he said. 'Pull.'

The black stallion tossed his head, his massive chest swelled as he backed. The rope became taut. The body of Pat was drawn slowly from the swamp.

Johnson patted the horse's neck as he dismounted. 'Slowly, boy,' he said. 'Slowly.'

He ran to the edge of the mud again and as Blackie continued to pull, gently steered the body on to dry land. It was not a pleasant task. Pat had been shot in the chest. Blood mingled with the stinking slime on his body. His face, which was comparatively clean, still wore that ludicrous, crumpled expression of surprise.

Johnson took the rope from the body and wiped it methodically on the grass. Then he returned it to its rightful place on the saddle of Pat's horse. He patted its flank, for its death had been the means of saving his bacon.

He picked up his dead pard's rifle once more and went to the base of the rocks where he had fallen. There he found his own Colt and sheathed it. He skirted the edge of the quagmire and began to climb towards the cluster of rocks where the bushwhacker had hidden.

He limped a little, and his bruised face was streaked with sweat and grime. He reached his objective, a semi-circle of rocks with a small grassy hollow in their midst: a perfect bushwhacker's nest. He went down on his knees and scrutinized the ground around him. He found Winchester shells: they were no use to him; a few cigarette-stubs, rolled weeds made from baccy and papers that could be gotten in any general store. The grass was flattened as if the man had lain there and waited.

Johnson rose and moved away from the spot. He found the place where the man's horse had stood. It was there he had his first real find. It was a plaited leather quirt with a lead-weighted handle. The bush-whacker had probably had it looped someplace on his saddle and in his haste to get away had not noticed that it had fallen. Johnson tucked it into his belt.

He began to descend the slope the other side, following the trail he figured the horse had used. He was almost on level ground when he saw the bunch of riders coming fast towards him.

He knew it was useless trying to get back over the hill before they saw him. They had probably already done so. With Pat's Winchester cradled in his arms he stood and waited.

The men came nearer. He did not know them but a few of their faces seemed familiar. At the head of them rode a stocky old man with iron-grey, slit eyes and a bitter mouth.

He said: 'What are you doin' on Triangle Plus land?'

'He's the new Curly Bar 6 ranny, boss,' said one of the men. Johnson suddenly recognized the latter: he had met him in the Billy Boy saloon in Sorrowful Creek the other night.

The old man grunted. Then he said harshly: 'Where's your hoss, young feller?'

Johnson jerked his thumb. 'The other side o' the hill.'

'Why ain't you with him – in your own territory?'

Johnson made the plunge. 'I got bushwhacked,' he said. He told them the whole tale.

There were exclamations from the men when they heard of the death of Pat but their boss said nothing, revealed no emotion whatsoever. Not until Johnson finished did he speak.

'Logan,' he said, and one of the men came forward. The boss took a pair of binoculars from his saddle and handed them over. 'Go to the top of the hill and have a look.'

'Sure, boss.' The man dismounted and climbed the hill. The others watched him. Nobody spoke. The man disappeared over the crown of the hill. All eyes were turned towards Johnson. Some were openly hostile, others curious. None were friendly. Those of the boss were mere slits. They revealed nothing.

Logan reappeared. He skidded down the hill, bringing a shower of loose shale with him. He began to talk breathlessly before he reached the bottom.

'It's right what he says, boss. Pat's down there – an' a coupla hosses an' a calf. Pat's lyin' on his back covered in mud an' blood. He looks mighty dead to me.'

'Did you see this bushwhacker?' said the boss, turning to Johnson. There was a faint sneer in the man's voice.

'I had a glimpse of him that's all. He was a tall feller.'

'A tall feller, uh?'

'Yeh, he must've been lying in wait for us.'

'Yeh, he must've been waitin' for yuh knowing you'd get to that swamp just at that time so's he could take potshots at yuh.'

Johnson said: 'He must've been watching us ride across the range. He must've moved into a good position as we got nearer.'

'Maybe he even watched you leave the ranch house, uh?'

'Yeh, maybe he had a pair o' binoculars.' As soon as he had said that Johnson knew he had said the wrong thing.

The other man's body stiffened. His small bitter mouth went tighter than ever. There was a pregnant silence. Then he said: 'I guess mebbe we oughta find a convenient tree an' string you up right now, younker.'

'What for?'

'We don't cotton on to bushwhackers in these parts. Particularly those who shoot their own riding-pards.'

There was a sullen murmur from some of the men behind him.

'So that's the way it lies is it?' said Johnson.

'That's the way it lies, younker.'

'You ain't even bin down the other side to look around.'

The beginning of a smile creased the older man's face. 'I don't trespass on my neighbour's territory.'

'Why would I want to trespass on your territory, leaving my horse back there, unless I was looking for something.'

'You've got a point there, younker. Did you find anythin'?'

Johnson did not hesitate. 'No.'

'You'd better drop that rifle, younker.'

Johnson hesitated. He could shoot the old man. But he knew the man called Logan was behind him.

He shrugged and let the rifle fall. The old man made a motion with his head. One of the men dismounted. At the same time cold steel was jabbed into Johnson's back.

The voice of Logan said: 'Hold still, pardner.' The hand of Logan took Johnson's gun from its holster.

The man who had dismounted picked up the rifle and handed it to his boss. The old man broke it open.

'That's Pat's rifle,' said Johnson. 'Like I told you, it ain't bin fired.'

'You're right there, younker.' The old man smiled his twisted bitter smile once more. 'Mebbe that's a point in your favour – maybe it ain't . . . Git a rope and tie his wrists,' he said.

Johnson started a little. 'Keep still,' snarled Logan and jabbed him again.

Another man, a lariat swinging in his hand, dismounted and joined the one who had taken the rifle. The two of them advanced on Johnson.

The pressure of the gun was taken from the yellow-haired young man's spine. He glanced over his shoulder. Logan was standing grinning with the gun dangling in his hand.

The two men came forward swiftly. Johnson ducked as the one who was empty-handed tried to grab him. He figured they were too close now for Logan to risk doing any shooting. He flung a blow, which hit his first attacker and knocked him spinning. The second one jumped out of the way just in time and swung the coiled rope. It whistled through the air and lashed Johnson's arms. He spun away, half-turning. Out of the corner of his eye he saw that Logan had come nearer, saw the glint of metal. He tried to dodge. The gun-barrel caught him a glancing blow on the side of the head. As he swayed his arms were pulled roughly behind him and lashed tightly with the rope.

The other end of the rope was hitched to the cantle of Logan's saddle.

'March, younker,' said the old man in a mocking voice.

TEN

Sorrowful Creek was just beginning to bustle with life as the cavalcade moved into the main drag. Store-keepers and their customers stood in the sunshine. They stared and greeted the Triangle Plus men. The latter answered them rather surreptitiously. Their boss rode at their head and did not look either to the right or the left.

A little to the rear of the boss rode Logan. Behind Logan was a long narrow lane between the ranks of men. At the end of this lane and at the other end of the rope which was tied to Logan's saddle, walked the man who called himself Bert Johnson.

He walked erect and his face was set. He did not seem to heed anything around him. He was like a man in a dream.

The cavalcade halted outside the sheriff's office. It was then that Johnson lurched. While he was walking he had kept going. But now it was evident he was dead-beat.

Bart Gaylord came out of his office and stopped dead on the boardwalk.

'Mr Browning,' he said. 'What's this?'

The old man, Ep Browning, said: 'Git back in there, sheriff, we've got a prisoner for yuh.'

Gaylord backed slowly. He was big and fancy but at that moment he looked a little at loss.

Ep Browning dismounted. 'You come with me, Logan,' he said. 'An' bring the prisoner . . . The rest of yuh stay here.'

The three men, the last one dragging at the end of a rope, passed into the office. The door closed behind them.

The curious townsfolk mingled with the Triangle Plus boys and began to ask questions. The boys seemed a little at loss themselves and none of them were very voluble. But pretty soon the Sorrowful Creek folks were due to see something else to set their tongues wagging.

This happened when two more Triangle Plus men rode down the main drag. Two men. Four horses. One horse, a magnificent black stallion, was riderless. The other carried a long shapeless bundle. Matted red hair, big hands dangling limply, boots swinging.

A youth ran alongside the grim quartet and, bending double, looked closer at the body.

'It's Pat O'Fallon!' he yelled. 'It's big Pat!'

As one man the rubbernecks turned away from the sheriff's office and streamed to meet this new sensation.

Meanwhile, inside the jail, Bert Johnson was shepherded brutally along the passage by George. The gangling deputy had not forgotten this stranger's treatment of him the last time they met and he took it

108

out of Johnson's back with his gun-barrel before he finally shoved him into a cell and locked the door.

Johnson slumped on to the bunk. His body drooped with weariness, but the look in his queer blue eyes as he lifted his head made George scuttle away with trepidation knocking at his heart.

From the stone wall beside the man on the bunk came a quick tap-tap. Johnson rose slowly. His feet dragged as he crossed to the barred door. He pressed the side of his face against the cold steel. It was soothing; he could also see a section of another face, the face of his neighbour in the next cell.

'What they got you for, Bert?' said Steve Lasare.

'Same as you,' said Johnson. 'I'll tell you all about it later. Have you got a cigarette?'

'Yeh.' Steve's hand came through the bars, holding a lighted cigarette. 'Can you reach it?'

Johnson reached out and took the cigarette. 'Thanks, Steve,' he said. 'Hang on, pardner. I'll see you later.'

'All right.'

Johnson moved away from the door. He sat down on the bunk and took deep drags at the soothing weed.

He finished it and ground the stub beneath his heel. Then he lay on his back on the bunk and went to sleep.

He awoke when somebody rattled his cell-door. The light was failing. The sheriff stood at the bars. 'You're a cool customer,' he said.

'Where's my hoss?' said Johnson.

'It ain't your hoss you ought to be thinkin' about now, young fellow.'

'Where is he?'

'He's in the stables out back. They brought him in. And Pat's body. Where did you throw the Winchester you shot him with, Johnson?'

'You can't pin that on me, Sheriff, no more than you can pin the other raps on Steve here.'

'You two are in league. Why are you here? What's your game?'

Johnson ignored the quick-fire questions. 'Everybody knows I rode from the ranch with Pat lookin' for strays.'

'So?' said Gaylord. 'You could have gone on in front of him pretending to chase a calf or something. You could've lain in wait. That's what you did, wasn't it? Pat never had a chance.'

The prisoner refused to be prodded. 'I didn't take a rifle with me, my Winchester's still underneath my bunk back at the ranch. Maybe I used Pat's, uh?'

'Smart,' said the sheriff. 'I know you didn't use Pat's. It hasn't been fired for a couple of days. You could have had one stashed someplace.'

'Up on them bluffs maybe. An' then I led Pat up there to be killed. That's slim reasonin' ain't it, Sheriff? You'll hafta do better than that – or look for another scapegoat. I've never seen such a durn' dressed-up an' useless lawman.'

The thrust went home – hard. Gaylord's face paled beneath his glorious crop of whiskers. His eyes were murderous. He said:

'I'll see that you an' your damn pard swing high.' He turned. His heels went clackety-clack as he went off down the passage.

'He sounds kinda het-up about sump'n,' drawled

Steve Lasare from the other cell. 'The stuffed-up, pansy-faced jackass. What goes on around here, Bert? I don't even know what the place looks like.'

Briefly Johnson told him what had transpired that morning. When he had finished Steve said: 'Somebody suttinly seems to have it in for the Curly Bar 6. Have you any idea who's behind it all?'

'I've got suspicions. A helluva lot of suspicions. Yet none seem to lead me any place – 'cept maybe this cell. It all started 'fore we got here, Steve.'

'He cain't hold us here. He ain't got enough evidence.'

'He was flummoxed before we came. A coupla strangers in the territory – actin' suspicious-like to boot – were manna from heaven to him.'

'My, you do talk eddicated at times,' said Steve. 'But I get your drift, pardner.'

The little man passed another lighted weed along. They smoked in silence, both deep in thought. It was almost dark. Even if they got right up against the bars they could not see each other's faces now, only the red glowing ends of the cigarettes.

George came into the passage and lit the swinging hurricane lantern.

'My, my, such luxury!' said Steve. 'How 'bout sump'n to eat, pardner?'

'You'll get it,' snarled George.

'Tough boy,' said Steve as the man withdrew. 'The sheriff shore ain't got much taste in deppities.'

'Only a half-wit like George would stand the blowed-up jackass so long I guess,' said Johnson.

A few moments later the half-wit in question

brought a tray. On it were two cups of muddy-grey liquid, two basins of muddy liquid of a rather lighter hue, knives and forks, and two noggins of bread.

'Ah, a feast for the gods,' said Steve.

George scowled and placed the tray on the floor in the middle of the passage. Then he drew his gun.

'Keep in the back there,' he snarled. 'If either of yuh make a move I'll let yuh have it.'

'All right, son,' said Steve. 'Jist give up the eats.'

George screwed his face up into a ferocious expression as he passed the little man's portion under the cell-door. He then did the same for Johnson. He waved his gun at them, with a last murderous look, scuttled off down the passage. Johnson smelled the cup of grey liquid, then the basin of lighter-grey liquid. One was coffee, the other stew, but it was a little difficult to determine which was which. Steve was having the same difficulty. He said: 'This is all I've had since I got clapped intuh this place. It's jist slops from a hash-house down the street.'

The little man did not sound so good-humoured now. He raised his voice. 'George,' he bawled. 'George.'

The door at the end of the passage opened. 'What's all the ruckus about,' came the deputy's plaintive voice.

'Come here, George,' said Steve a little more softly. Johnson listened tensely. He knew his pard of old. Right now he did not like the tone of Steve's voice.

George's footsteps shuffled. His lean shadow was thrown on the opposite wall. Johnson heard Steve cross the cell. He could see George as he halted in his old position, before the cell but in the centre of the passage. Then Steve said: 'What's this stuff in this yere cup, George?'

'It's cawfee. What d'yuh think it is?' George sounded aggrieved. His lean, weak-chinned face became puckered comically with indignation.

Steve's reactions were sudden and violent. 'Taste it then,' he said.

A stream of muddy-grey liquid hit George full in the face. He howled and staggered back. The steaming liquid matted his lank hair across his forehead, streamed down his face and over his shirt-front. He knuckled his eyes like a crying child, his lips yammered, half incoherent curses spilling from them. He groped frenziedly for his gun. Finally he got it out and waved it while he mopped his face with the sleeve on his other arm.

'I'll kill you,' he screamed. 'I'll kill you!'

He took his sleeve away from his eyes and sheer hate and naked murder blazed there. He was mad with fury. Johnson ran to his cell door as George levelled the gun at Steve.

'Stop it, you crazy fool!' yelled the yellow-haired man.

The door at the end of the passage crashed open. Sheriff Gaylord stormed in.

'What the hell's goin' on? George. . . !'

George turned, the gun wavering. In three more strides Gaylord was upon him. He snatched the gun from his hand. Then he gave him a stinging slap across the face which sent him spinning back against the wall.

George cowered there and rubbed his cheek. His

eyes were wide and scared. He looked on the point of blubbering.

'He threw coffee all over me, sheriff,' he bleated.

'Watch yourself, George,' said Gaylord. 'Get back in the office.'

The deputy slunk along the wall like a whipped cur until he had passed his boss. Then he scuttled off. The door slammed behind him.

Gaylord weighted the gun in his hand. His face was white, vicious and rat-like beneath the lamplight, despite its luxuriant camouflage. He reached to the back of his belt and brought forth his keys. With these in one hand and the levelled gun in the other he crossed the passage and opened Steve's door. Then he passed out of Johnson's sight.

The yellow-haired ranny pressed himself against the barred door of his cell. He heard Steve curse, the sheriff say, 'Don't try it. Don't try it—' Then there was a scuffle, a smack, another smack, and a thud. Footsteps passed across the stone floor once more. The door rattled. The sheriff came into view, the gun still dangling in his hand.

'You yeller-livered skunk,' said the usually phlegmatic Johnson. 'What've you done to him?'

The sheriff did not speak. He did not turn round. He went on down the passage and the door banged behind him with a terrible finality.

There was silence in the cell-block. Then Johnson said 'Steve.'

There was no answer. He rattled the door. 'Steve,' he said again.

Steve's voice came back to him. It was a little weak.

'It's all right, pardner. He jist slugged me a coupla times. I'll be all right in a minute. It'll take more than a panty-waist like him to lay *me* low.'

Steve stopped talking then. His neighbour heard him drag himself across the floor, reach the bunk, haul himself up on it. It creaked beneath his weight. Then there was silence again.

Johnson was overtaken by a terrible sense of frustration, a blinding rage which he tried to kill but which tore through his solid body like a consuming flame. He began to pace the cell and strike his fist into the palm of his hand. The food which had been brought to him stood unnoticed beneath his bunk. None of the things he felt showed on his fleshy expressionless face, but his light-blue eyes gleamed with a strange, almost insane light.

He stopped his pacing when Steve's voice came to him again.

'Great Jesophat, I a'most wish I hadn't wasted that coffee. I shore could do with it now.'

'If you hadn't wasted the coffee you wouldn't've needed it,' Johnson told him.

'You got a point there, pardner. What's the stew like?'

'I haven't tasted it.'

Steve fell silent again. He was probably sampling the stew. The little Texan had the constitution of a young bull. Johnson sat down and broke bread into his own stew. He sampled it. It was pretty awful but better than nothing at all. He sipped the coffee, spat out a mouthful and slung the rest at the cell wall. He wished it had been himself who had drenched George.

A few moments later George came into the passage and blew out the hurricane-lantern.

'We ain't wastin' no oil on you skunks,' he said out of the darkness.

'Go an' boil your head, yuh skinny freak,' said Steve wearily.

George made a sound like a cat spitting. He stomped off down the passage and banged the door behind him.

'Wal,' said Steve. 'I think I'll get me some shuteye.'

Johnson could sense the pain behind his light tones, the rage he felt against Sheriff Gaylord. The little Texan had more guts in his little finger than that big faker had in the whole of his dressed-up body. Johnson said: 'Goodnight.'

Steve's reply was a sleepy grunt.

Johnson lay on his back and composed himself for sleep, a thing he usually managed to do, no matter what the circumstances. He had slept in worse places than this jail, on harder beds than this bunk with its lumpy horse-hair mattress. But somehow tonight sleep just would not come. Maybe that was because he had slept so deeply that afternoon . . . Yet, deep inside of him, he knew that was not the real reason.

He turned over on his side and almost fell off the narrow bunk. He turned the other way and faced the cold wall. Some half-hope made him rise and climb up on the bunk. He reached up and jerked at the iron bars of the small grating. They were firmly set and, even if they were not, even if there were no bars there, he could not get his broad body through that small gap. Was he going crazy? He got down and sat on the edge of the bunk. It was then he heard the sound.

It was undefinable at first, a mere something impinging on his keyed-up senses. Then gradually it took form and meaning. It was the sound of soft footfalls advancing slowly down the passage.

Johnson rose. There was something unutterably sinister about that slowly growing sound, little more than the scratching of a rat in a barn as he gnawed through some object which barred his way, coming nearer all the time. Was this the finish of it all, thought Johnson. Was this the big pay-off? The shot in the night. The body dragged from the cell. The sheriff's plea of a violent, escaping prisoner. It had been done before . . .

There was a shadowy form, a glint of metal. Johnson braced himself, tried to dissolve in the shadows.

A voice called his name softly. A voice he recognized. His own voice was surprised as he answered. A key rattled in the lock. The door swung open and Johnson crossed slowly towards it. He was still wary.

'Slim,' he said.

Slim said: 'Hurry up. You're getting out of here.'

'Where're the sheriff an' his deputy?'

'The sheriff's down at the Billy Boy celebratin' his big coup. The deputy's asleep in the office, in the darkness. He's liable to be asleep quite a while. He didn't see who hit him. It ain't like you to talk so much, Johnson. Come on, get moving.'

He stepped aside. Johnson went past him and in front of him. Slim shut the cell-door and locked it.

'I like to leave everything nice an' tidy,' he said. He moved up behind Johnson.

Cold water ran down Johnson's spine. His body was tense.

117

ELEVEN

He said: 'How about my pard in the next cell? Let him out.'

Slim said: 'The Ol' Man said to get you out. He didn't say nothin' about anybody else.'

'Oh, it was the Ol' Man was it? What's his game?'

'Search me,' said Slim. He sounded unusually flippant. Then his voice roughened. 'Come on, don't talk so much – an' get movin'. I don't want nobody jumping me on this hop.'

Johnson turned in the darkness to face him and stood still.

'I ain't movin' till you get my pard out,' he said. 'That skunk of a sheriff has manhandled him once tonight. He'll take it out of him again when he finds out I've been sprung. He'll probably beat him up to try to make him talk.'

From the other cell came the grumbling of Steve's voice as he awoke.

Then he burbled: 'Whaddi you say, Bert?'

'We're supposed to be in league,' hissed Johnson. 'I

119

don't go unless he does.'

'Whassat?' said Steve plaintively.

'Looks like I gotta take him,' said Slim in a furious whisper. 'But understand: once he's outside he's on his own. We've only got one spare hoss.'

He went back to Steve's cell and unlocked the door. Johnson followed him.

'Come on, pardner,' he said. 'Shake your pins. We're getting out o' this dump.'

'Gettin' out?' said Steve. His voice was unutterably weary.

Johnson crossed the cell and bent over him. 'Get up, Steve,' he said. 'Make it snappy. We're gettin' out I tell yuh.'

Steve began to get up slowly. Johnson felt for him in the dark, got his arm around his shoulders to help him. He realized then that his pard had been hurt worse than he had thought.

The little tubby man was lurching as Johnson helped him across to the door. Neither of them said anything. Slim closed the door and locked it. The three of them went along the passage.

Slim unlocked the back door with a key from the ring. He said: 'I cain't remember Gaylord ever havin' a jail break before. He ain't had many prisoners if it comes to that. It was like takin' candy from a kid.'

Outside a man waited with two horses. A gun glinted in Slim's hand as he turned. He pointed it at Steve.

'You'd better make your own way now, friend,' he said.

'He's comin' with us,' said Johnson. 'He can get up in

120

front o' my hoss.' He paused as Slim stood a little uncertainly. Then he said: 'Where's the stable attached to the jail?'

'Over there.' Slim pointed. 'Hey, where you going you crazy fool? Come back here,' he hissed.

'My hoss's in there,' whispered Johnson, turning. 'I gotta get him.'

Slim said: 'The Ol' Man certainly wished a pile o' trouble on me.' He turned to his companion, young Locus. 'Watch this bozo,' he said, jerking a thumb at Steve.

Locus patted his gun-barrel. 'Awlright,' he said. 'Stay right there, fat boy.'

Steve said: 'Jist let me lean on this hoss. I'm mighty tired – mighty tired.'

He suited the action to his words. Locus drew his gun. But Steve was still now, his head resting on the horse's saddle. He seemed to have fallen asleep.

Slim cat-footed after Johnson. He paused behind him at the stable door. 'Now what?' he said in a furious whisper.

'It's padlocked.'

'You'll have to leave it then. That depitty's liable to wake up any minute.'

'I'm not gonna high-tail without Blackie.'

'You talk of that hoss as if he's a human bein'.'

'To me he's worth a dozen o' some folks I've met.'

'Yeh,' said Slim softly. 'He's a good hoss. I know how you feel. But – he's your hoss not mine an' I ain't stickin' my neck out for him any longer.'

Johnson tensed as the cold barrel of the gun was jabbed into his back. Slim went on: 'I aim to do what I came here for, I ain't leavin' without you. An' we're goin' right now. Air yuh comin' quietly or do I hafta slug yuh an' pile you on a hoss?'

To be taken away like that, without knowing what, was going on was the last thing Johnson wanted. Besides, he had been slugged enough for one day. His head still ached from the smack Logan, the Triangle Plus man, had given him.

'Slim,' he said. 'Just another second. Lend me that gun will yuh?'

Slim chuckled deep in his throat. 'You take the biscuit. I give you my gun an' leave muhself wide open. What d'yuh aim to do: blow the lock off an' bring all the town on our ears?'

'No, this lock ain't very strong. I figure I could bust it open with a gun-barrel.'

Slim chuckled again. 'We're gabbin' here an' we ain't thought to try one o' the keys on the ring.' He jangled it. 'Get back, Bert,' he said. 'Go on, back up!'

Johnson backed away. One by one Slim tried the keys in the lock. Finally there was a click. The door flew open. There was a snort from inside. Slim backed away but he was not quick enough. He was sent sprawling by the horse.

'Blackie,' said Johnson.

The horse stopped, pawing the ground. Johnson darted forward and picked up Slim's gun. The young ramrod got up. He looked at the gun in Johnson's hand. He shrugged.

'I figured you for a four-flusher,' he said. 'But I hoped I was wrong.'

'I'm just careful,' said Johnson. 'There's a lot o'

things I cain't figger. Carry on as planned – but this time I'll carry the gun.'

'I got yuh out didn't I—?'

'Go on,' said Johnson. He made a clicking noise with his tongue and Blackie followed them.

Locus peered into the darkness. 'Put that gun away, kid,' said Johnson. 'We don't want any shootin'.'

'Do as he says,' put in Slim.

Locus slowly holstered his gun.

Blackie had not been unsaddled. Johnson climbed up on his back.

'Git up there, Steve,' he said. 'Let's get going.'

With a grunt of weariness the little Texan came alive. He climbed on to the back of the horse the two men had brought for Johnson.

Johnson said: 'You'd better take the lead, Slim.'

Slim said nothing. He went in front. 'What's goin' on?' said Locus.

'Quiet!' The young man did not like Johnson's tone. He was a new Johnson. The gun in his hand was ominously steady. Locus shrugged and became quiet.

They left the ashcans and the rubbish heaps of the town behind. Slim rode without hesitation. He followed no obvious trail, just plunged on across the grassland. Finally Johnson realized they were on Curly Bar 6 land, and approaching the brush where Pat had been killed. However, Slim skirted this and plunged on. Everybody was silent. Johnson shot glances from time to time at his little pard. Steve was slumped over his horse's neck. He seemed to have gone to sleep again.

They reached a three-strand wire fence, silver

threads in the night, rather a rarity in cattle-country. As they passed alongside this Slim dropped back and rode behind Johnson.

The young ramrod said: 'This is the Triangle Plus boundary. Ol' Ep Brownin' had this fence put up a coupla years ago. Said he was losing calves, said they were comin' over here an' our boys were brandin' 'em. The boys wanted to go an' take his place apart. Might've bin a range-war. The Ol' Man stopped it, sent a message for Ep to get on with his fencing. The Ol' Man was right I reckon, no use havin' blood shed over a thing like that. Guess he wouldn't've been like that in his younger days though.'

The fence ended at a craggy knob of a hill which rose suddenly out of the grasslands like a giant fist.

'We call this the Big Boy's Fist,' said Slim. 'It's the end of the range. The territory for a few miles past it ain't good for nothing 'cept coyotes an' gophers.'

He veered his horse suddenly and its hoofs clattered on hard rock. Then at the base of the fist-like rock Johnson saw a small tumble-down cabin. The bunch reined in front of it. Slim said: 'This is our furthest line-hut an' it ain't used much. Will you trust me to go inside fust an' light the lamp, Bert?' His voice was sardonic.

'All right. I'll trust yuh.'

Johnson dismounted and stood outside the door. Steve jerked erect and said: 'Where are we?'

Locus grunted: 'I know where you oughta be – both of yuh. Nolly's makin' turkey soup tonight an' I'm mighty hungry. There probably won't be any left when we get back.'

Inside the cabin light blossomed. It streamed through the door as Slim opened it wider. 'Come on in,' he said.

'After you,' said Johnson to Locus.

The younker got down from his horse and swaggered in front. He was followed by Steve who seemed to find it difficult to walk straight. When Johnson followed the little tubby man into the cabin he realized why. One side of Steve's face and his one temple was a bruised and bloodied mess.

The little man crossed the room and sat down on the bunk at the back. The only other articles of furniture consisted of a small deal table and two rickety kitchen chairs. To the right of the table was a pot-bellied stove with a sagging pipe which went up through a hole in the roof. The cabin had one window which was covered entirely by a dirty old blanket.

Johnson said: 'My pardner's sick. He wants sump'n put inside of him, an' that face fixed.'

'Who did that?' said Slim.

'Gaylord.'

Slim cursed savagely. Steve sat on the bunk, silent, with his head hanging now, as if he was ashamed to show his face.

Locus said: 'I've got a bottle of whiskey in my saddlebag. I'll go get it.'

'Gimme your gun, pardner,' said Johnson.

Locus glared at him. 'Give it to him,' said Slim. 'We don't want any trouble. If he wants to be so damn' suspicious there's nothin' we can do about it.'

Locus scowled and handed over his gun. He went outside and a few moments later returned with a bottle half full of whiskey. From a small cupboard in a corner Slim produced a tin cup. Johnson took the whiskey, poured a stiff tot and carried it to Steve.

'Knock that back, pardner,' he said.

Steve looked up. His battered face twisted in a travesty of a smile. His luxurious moustache was bedraggled. He took the cup and tossed it back. He squinted his eyes.

'Thanks,' he said. 'I shore needed that.'

Locus, under orders from Slim, was lighting the fire. He went outside again and returned with an armful of wood.

'Plenty round back,' he said. 'Under some corrugated sheeting.'

From the cupboard Slim took a small saucepan. 'There's a small stream out back too,' he said. 'I'll go get some water an' you can bathe your pard's face. I guess we cain't turn him out now, but what the Ol' Man's gonna say when he hears about it I dunno.'

Johnson opened his mouth to say something. But Slim had already gone. He returned with the saucepan, full of water, and placed it atop the stove in which Locus already had a fire roaring.

He said: 'You're bein' treated like lords.'

Johnson said: 'What's the Ol' Man's game? Why does he want me here?'

'That I don't know.'

'Does *he* think I killed Pat an' he's figuring to make me confess the rest an' tell him why.'

'He doesn't think you killed Pat. He's holdin' Gil Pendexter for it.'

'Gil Pendexter?'

126

'Yeh, he swore to get even with Pat after that ruckus they had in the mess-hut that first night you got here. He rode out alone after the two of you this morning. He didn't wait for orders. Then later, two o' the boys met him comin' back on the edge of the brush . . . It wasn't till later that we heard about the death o' Pat an' that you'd been raked in for it. Gaylord came to the ranch house an' crowed over the Ol' Man. The Ol' Man took it quieter than I expected him to. But, as soon as the sheriff had gone he had Pendexter in the office an' questioned him. Pendexter said he'd been looking for strays, he hadn't heard no shots, he hadn't seen nothin'. Whether he killed Pat or not he did wrong ridin' off without orders. What the Ol' Man is actually drivin' at I ain't the one to figure, but he's had Pendexter locked in one o' the stables.'

'What did he tell you to do?'

'Jest what I did. I was to get you outa jail an' bring you here. He didn't offer no explanation an', knowing him, I didn't ask for any.'

'Jest like that, uh?' said Johnson.

'Yeh,' said Slim. Then: 'If we could have our guns back now, Bert. We've got to ride. You'll be safe here I guess.' Johnson did not move. Slim went on: 'Look, I'll show you sump'n.' He crossed the room to the bunk. 'Can you get up, friend?' Steve got up.

Slim caught hold of the side of the bunk and lifted it wholesale away from the wall. He then drew away two loose upright logs, leaving an aperture wide enough to take a man's body. He said:

'This part of the cabin backs flush on to the Big

Boy's Fist. It ain't generally known but in that pesky hill is an old mine-working. A couple of crazy prospectors started a-diggin' here a good many years back. I don't think they found anything. I've heard tell, by some of the older boys when I first joined the Curly Bar 6, that one o' these prospectors was a pard o' the Ol' Man's. He got killed. Maybe that's why the Ol' Man had this cabin built – sort of in memory of him.'

'I wouldn't give him credit for that much sentiment,' said Johnson.

'No, maybe not. Anyway, this gap leads into the mine-workings. If you get jumped you can get out through this tunnel. It bores upwards an' comes out somewhere on the slopes of Big Boy's Fist.'

Slim backed again, replaced the logs and put the bunk back into its old position. Steve sat on it again.

Slim said: 'I don't know what the Ol' Man's drivin' at – 'cept mebbe he don't like havin' none of his boys in jail – but he's evidently trustin' yuh. Nobody's tryin' to keep yuh here least of all me an' Locus, seein' as you've got both the guns.'

'Yeh, I've got both the guns.'

'Tell you what I'll do,' said Slim. 'You give my pard his gun back an' you can hang on to mine. Mebbe you'll need it.'

'All right,' said Johnson. He gave Locus his gun back.

Slim said: 'All right. Come on.' At the door he turned.

'I hope we'll see you again, Bert.' After that last

128

cryptic remark he and Locus vanished. Their horses clattered away into the night and then there was silence.

TWELVE

Johnson crossed to the cupboard in the corner. He found three cans of pork and beans. Also a can-opener – and something else he needed: a small basin. There was a collection of tin plates and mugs and rather battered knives and forks.

Back to the table Johnson took the small earthenware basin, a can of beans, two tin plates and a couple of forks. The saucepan of water on the stove was boiling merrily. He took it off and poured the water into the basin. He dragged the table nearer to the bunk on which the unusually taciturn Steve sat motionless.

Johnson took a grubby white kerchief from his pocket and soaked it in the water.

'It's the best I can do for the moment, pardner,' he said.

'It ain't nothin' to worrit over, Bert,' said Steve.

'It ain't purty either. It's gotta be fixed.'

Johnson scalded the kerchief well and rung it out. 'Lie back,' he said.

Steve lay back and the would-be medico bathed the face well. He said: 'We ought to have some ointment or

somethin' . . . That Slim, he's gone off, he ain't bother-
ing . . .'

'Who is he?'

'The ramrod at the spread I work for.'

'What's his angle?'

'I don't know,' said Johnson slowly. 'I don't know.
Things are stackin'-up a little too fast for me lately.'

He became silent as he finished his job. 'Did that
young geezer leave any o' that whiskey?' said Steve.

Johnson gave one of his rare chuckles. 'There ain't
much wrong with you now,' he said. 'Yeh, there's half a
cupful here.' He passed it over. The little Texan quaffed
it with relish. Then he combed his luxurious black
moustache out with his fingers.

'Could you do with some chow?' said Johnson.
'Beans?'

'Yeh, even beans!'

Johnson left the cabin and felt his way around the
back to the trickle of the stream which came right out
of the solid rock. The night was very black, very silent.
After he had filled the saucepan he stood for a while,
looking around him, thinking deeply.

Was he being foolish hanging around here now? Had
he overplayed his hand? Perhaps it would be better to
light out pronto while they still had a chance? What
sort of game were the Old Man and Slim playing? Why
hadn't they wanted Steve to come along with him? The
jail break seemed to have gone very smoothly – too
damn' smoothly. Slim had been too cocky and too easily
led, the reverse of his usually fiery self. What was the
meaning of it all? Was this the end of the trail? – a hell
of a different ending to the one he had planned!

The questions buzzed around in his brain. His eyes were becoming accustomed to the darkness. He looked behind him, looked upwards at the knobbly black outlines of the Big Boy's Fist. He looked at the corner of the cabin which was built flush with a rock. What a cute trick that had been! He looked the other way, out into the void of the sky mingling with the gently-breathing grasslands. And, as he did so, a new daring plan and the beginning of a theory began to form themselves in his mind.

He took the saucepan of water and went back into the cabin. He made up the fire and put the water atop the stove. He punched the top of the can of beans and stood the can in the water.

Steve was half asleep, a cigarette dangling from his lips. He handed the packet to Johnson. The latter took a weed and lit up. Both men were silent, Steve half dozing, Johnson sitting on a chair and looking fixedly at the hot stove, no vestige of expression on his face.

The beans started to bubble. He took off his hat and crumpled it to catch hold of the hot can. He opened the can and served the beans. Steve awoke with a jerk and rose. He crossed to the table and drew up a chair.

'Shove 'em over here, pardner,' he said.

'Certainly, suh,' said Johnson with grave mockery. He knew that Steve was being flippant again to disguise how badly he was hurt. The wounded side of his face glowed beneath the light. It was a mass of torn red flesh and purple bruises.

Steve finished off his beans and had another plate-ful. After mopping that up he said: 'Wal, now I guess I'll get some shuteye. I don't know what all this is about but I don't aim to do no worrittin'.'

He went over to his bunk and lay down. 'Call me at noon tomorrow,' he said. Then he suddenly jerked erect.

'Hey! Where are you gonna sleep?'

'I ain't tired. Don't you worry about me. Lie down, yuh little skunk.'

'Wal, if you put it that way.' Steve subsided again. A few moments later he was snoring.

Johnson went across to him and gently took the packet of cigarettes out of his vest pocket. The little man did not stir. That was a sure sign that he was beat to the wide. Johnson went back to the table. He lit a cigarette. Then he turned out the lamp and sat in the darkness, smoking.

He must have dozed; he awoke with a start. There was something he had to do! – and according to his figuring it must be almost dawn.

Steve was still snoring. Johnson rose quietly, a little stiffly. He opened the door and went outside. He closed the door softly behind him.

He discovered Blackie cropping the grass a few yards away. He mounted him and urged him gently forward. The horse seemed to understand that stealth was needed. His hoofbeats were muffled. Not until they were some distance away from the cabin did Johnson urge him into a gallop.

Finally they reached the swamp where Pat had died. The bluffs rising above it were dark against the slowly lightening sky. Johnson left Blackie and began to climb.

He went right over the top of the ridge and down the other side. Then he looked about him, getting his bearings. He moved to the right, went a little lower. He stopped again. Here he had stood when Ep Browning and his men rode down upon him. He had moved a little lower then, to that cluster of rocks. He went to the cluster of rocks, moved among them. He bent and picked up the quirt he had dropped there. It was lucky he had had the presence of mind to do so. He tucked the fancy lead-weighted, leather-thonged thing into his belt. Then he retraced his steps.

As he forked Blackie and turned his head in the direction of the cabin, dawn was pearling the edges of the hills and there was a gentle morning breeze.

He rode hard.

The morning light was stronger when he reached his objective. The cabin was still and cold. He was surprised to find the door was a little ajar. He reached for his gun as he pushed it open. The place was empty. The clothes were tumbled on the bunk but there was no sign of Steve. Johnson went outside again, went around the back. Then he returned and went out on to the edge of the range. Steve's horse had gone. He squinted his eyes; in the grey light a horseman was coming towards him.

Johnson stood undecided for a moment. Then he turned and went back into the cabin. He went to the window and pulled the curtain a little aside. He drew his gun and waited.

The horseman came nearer. Johnson recognized Slim. He holstered his gun and went to the door. Slim dismounted and came towards the cabin. He carried a small burlap sack over his shoulder. He said: 'I've brought you some eats.'

Johnson did not say anything but stepped aside to let him pass. Slim did so, rather warily. Then he halted. 'Where's your pardner?'

'I dunno. He's gone. I was just goin' to look for him.'

Slim put the sack on the table. 'Have you been out of the cabin?'

'Yeh. He'd gone when I came back.'

'That's awkward,' said Slim. 'The Ol' Man's comin' here.'

'When?'

'Any time now.'

'Why?'

'Don't ask me that, pardner.'

'I am askin' yuh.'

'Wal, the answer is: I don't know.'

'I ain't waitin' around for him nor nobody else,' said Johnson. 'I gotta find Steve. He might think I've run out on him. He's a bull-headed little cuss. I know him – he ain't takin' that beatin' he had last night so lightly as he appears to. He's out on the rampage on his lonesome I'll betcha.'

Slim's eyes suddenly blazed. 'If he's the bushwhacker – an' the Ol' Man out on his lonesome . . . if I know him he will be—'

'Steve's no bushwhacker,' said Johnson. 'I'm goin' after him an' you'd better not try an' stop me.'

'I'm comin' with yuh,' said Slim. Then he added softly: 'I wish I could really trust you, Bert. Who are you? What do yuh want?'

Johnson did not reply. He strode forward towards his horse. Slim looked at the broad back and dropped his hand to the butt of his gun. Then he shrugged and took it away again and followed Johnson. As he reached the man, who stood by his black stallion, Johnson had something in his hand. It was a riding quirt.

'Do you know who this belongs to, Slim?' he said.

Slim took it into his hands and scrutinized it. When he looked up his eyes were puzzled. 'Sure, I know who it belongs to, I could tell this fancy thing anywhere – there ain't no cowhands use a quirt like this – even if they use one at all. This is Sheriff Gaylord's. I've seen him whippin' his cayuse with it many a time. He seemed to like wavin' it around.'

'He waved it around once too often.'

'What do you mean, Bert? Where did you get this?'

'The bushwhacker who killed Pat, an' nearly got me too, dropped it as he ran away.'

Slim was still too dumbfounded to say anything; suspicion was dawning in his eyes.

Johnson went on: 'I caught a glimpse o' the feller. He was tall – even then I thought there was something familiar lookin' about him.'

'Did you see him drop it?'

'No, I didn't actually see him drop it—'

'But you saw the feller – a tall feller?' There was a queer note in Slim's voice.

'Yeh, I saw him all right . . . You don't believe me, do you?'

'What do you expect. . . ? I dunno what to believe. You say you saw the man – but you didn't recognize him. Maybe it was Gil Pendexter after all, he's tall an' thin—'

'How do you account for the sheriff's quirt bein' up there?'

137

'Don't ask me that.' Twice in the last few minutes Slim had used that phrase. He looked uncertain, a little suspicious.

Johnson said: 'Standin' gabbin' here won't do any good. An' it won't find Steve.'

He mounted Blackie. Slim forked his own mount and said: 'We'll ride back towards the ranch an' meet the Ol' Man.'

'We'll . . .' said Johnson and stopped. Then he shrugged. 'All right,' he said.

They rode across the range and hit the main trail to the Curly bar 6. The sun was beginning to break through the nearly morning haze. Both men looked around them as they rode. Visibility as yet was not very good but as far as they could see on three sides of them was the rolling plain and, behind them, the hills which were already vanishing in the haze. The only moving things were little bunches of grazing cattle.

A sense of urgency seemed to be impelling Slim forward. He raced his horse. Johnson kept up with him, but he kept looking around him anxiously. They were thundering down the trail and Slim had drawn a little way in front when they heard the shots.

Slim jerked so hard on the reins that his horse reared. The young ramrod looked back at Johnson. His face was set, his eyes blazed.

Johnson did not seem to notice the look, did not seem to realize the chance he was taking as he sent Blackie past Slim's horse.

'Come on,' he shouted.

Slim's reply was unintelligible. He spurred his horse viciously.

138

Johnson was flat over Blackie's neck when he saw the buckboard coming towards them. Its two horses were running madly. There was nobody on the driver's seat.

Johnson veered his horse to the side of the trail and slowed him down. Slim caught up with him.

'The boss!' he shouted. There was real anguish in his voice. And something like menace too.

The two horses came on at breakneck speed, the buckboard swaying from side to side behind them.

Johnson said: 'I'll take the other side. Move in when I shout.'

Slim nodded dumbly. Johnson urged Blackie to the other side of the trail.

He waited till the horses were almost abreast of them then he pressed Blackie with his knees and shouted, 'Now.'

As he flung himself from the saddle, he saw Slim doing the same from the other side. Both of them landed astride their objectives and the look of triumph they exchanged crushed out everything else for that pregnant second. Lying across the horse's back Johnson caught hold of the traces and hauled on them. 'Whoa,' he shouted. 'Whoa!' He could hear Slim yelling beside him.

Gradually the pace of the horses slackened. They were blowing and sweating when they finally drew to a halt. The condition of their riders was a little better.

They turned and swarmed back into the buckboard. It was empty.

'Back!' yelled Slim, almost frenziedly. 'Back!'

He leapt from the buckboard and mounted his

horse. Then he caught hold of the traces and turned the horses round to face back home. 'Get on,' he said. The horses began to trot back the way they had come.

Meanwhile Johnson had forked Blackie. The two riders thundered on, neck-and-neck, leaving the buckboard far behind.

On the trail in front of them a man lay on the ground and another one was bending over him. The second man was Steve Lasare. Slim cursed vilely, drew his gun, levelled it.

'Hold it, you crazy fool!' yelled Johnson. With a swing of his fist he knocked the gun from Slim's hand. It spun in the air and landed in the grass at the side of the trail.

Slim leapt from his horse and dived. Johnson went after him. He grabbed him just as the young ramrod had his hand on the gun once more. Slim tried to raise it. Johnson hit him hard in the belly then, as he doubled up, wrenched the gun from him and tucked it into his own belt.

Slim straightened up and lunged. There was murder in his eyes. Johnson swung his fist again. It was a perfectly balanced blow with all the weight of his heavy body behind it. It connected with Slim's jaw with a dull crack. The young ramrod went down and stayed down.

Johnson ran to his pard's side. Steve was nursing his shoulder. Blood seeped through his fingers. At his feet lay the Old Man. He was on his back and his eyes were closed.

THIRTEEN

'He's still alive,' said Steve. His bloodied face was white and strained. He spoke in jerky sentences. 'It was the sheriff an' his sidekick. Got him in the back. I almost caught 'em at it. I got George – he's over there in the grass. The sheriff got me in the shoulder – then he hightailed it—'

'Hang on, pardner,' said Johnson. He turned as the buckboard came rattling down the trail. The two horses halted as he stood in their path.

'Can you make it, pardner?' said Johnson.

Steve nodded. He climbed up on to the buckboard.

Johnson went down beside the Old Man. The pulse was very feeble. A groan from Slim made Johnson turn. The young ramrod was climbing to his feet.

Johnson ran across to him and helped him up. Slim's eyes blazed again. Johnson drew his gun and poked it at him.

'Listen, you damn' fool,' he said. He was no longer the phlegmatic, slow-talking cowhand. The very harshness and urgency of his tone, plus the menacing gun, made Slim quieten down.

Johnson told him, swiftly, what had happened, and finished by saying, 'The Ol' Man's badly hurt but he may have a chance. Help me to get him into the buckboard.'

'All right, Bert,' said Slim. 'You can put your gun away. '

Johnson holstered his Colt. They went over to the Old Man, gently lifted him and placed him on a pile of sacking in the back of the buckboard.

'Get up on that seat,' said Johnson. 'I'll go get what's left of that deppity.' Meekly Slim did as he was told.

Steve's shot had sent a slug clean between George's eyes. Johnson slung the body over his shoulder like a sack of meal and carried it back to the buckboard.

'Burn the wind to the ranch, Slim,' he said. 'I'm goin' after that sheriff.'

'He ain't got much of a start, Bert,' said Steve weakly. 'He seemed to be makin' f'r the hills.' He pointed.

Slim said: 'Mebbe I'd—'

'Get goin',' said Johnson and turned his horse's head. Slim whipped up the horses and the buckboard rattled off towards the Curly Bar 6. Johnson sent Blackie across the range in a breakneck gallop in the other direction. He hoped he had weighed the sheriff up right: a cold-blooded, calculated murderer, driven to do what he had done by some queer vanity or motive, but now panicky – unmasked, his little world on the verge of crashing around his ears, his only thought, escape!

As Johnson rode the morning wind whipped at his ears, blew strands of his long yellow hair which curled from beneath his Stetson. The sun was breaking and the haze had gone. The range before him was a shimmering sea of green. The hills were a deeper blue etched against the blue sky.

It was a peaceful morning, such a morning as that part of the country was famed for. But this man, who had carried vengeance in his heart through the years, a vengeance greater even than that which burned in him now, was oblivious to beauty and atmosphere. His horse was like a black demon beneath him, stretched, with ears back flat to his powerful head, in a long loping gallop. There had never been anything as fast as he on that range before – even Firecracker, who had been the king of the wild horses, had never been that fleet.

And the man leaning over the saddle, his face close to the horse's ear as if he was talking to him in some special language, seemed part of the horse himself. They were speed incarnate – and black vengeance.

And, when some time later, looking back, Bart Gaylord saw them on his tail, a look of baffled murderous rage transformed his weakly handsome face into a grotesquely-grinning mask. He knew now that he would not be able to approach the town as if nothing had happened and salvage whatever he could before the hounds came after him; he knew now that he must keep on for the hills and, if need be, turn, show his fangs and fight.

The distance between them gradually lessened. The sheriff's horse was a fast beast, but it could not compare with Blackie. The hills became nearer, nearer, crystal clear against the skyline, and the tall foppish rider with the goatee beard urged his horse to one last desperate effort.

The man's manner was panicky, his eyes gleamed insanely. He began to beat the horse about the ears with his fist. The beast, used to the sting of a loaded quirt, was bewildered and momentarily stunned. He stumbled as they passed into the brush at the base of the foothills. The man bawled insane curses into his ear and hit him again with his fist.

The horse lurched once more then turned and snapped at its rider. Gaylord's eyes almost started from his head. He lost all control. He let go of the reins and buffeted at the beast with both fists and screamed at him to go faster.

The horse, ill-treated for years, yet, in the manner of dumb beasts, still trusty, had had enough. It skidded to a halt and reared. It screamed. Its rider screamed too as he was pitched from the saddle. The horse snorted, tossed its head, and galloped away.

Gaylord extricated himself from the brush. 'Come back,' he shouted. 'Come back.' He shook his fists and then sent a stream of curses to high heaven. But the horse was never coming back. And with it had gone Gaylord's most treasured weapon, his Winchester repeater.

The man drew his gun and looked back. The black horse was coming at a terrible speed. Gaylord levelled his gun and fired. Then he turned to face the bluffs and began to run.

He broke through the brush, the hills before him. He turned again. The black horse was crashing through the brush now. The man on its back had a gun in his hand. He and the sheriff fired simultaneously.

A slug burned Gaylord's cheek and he knew, in the same instance, that he had missed. Panic overwhelmed him again and he turned, half-crouching, and lurched forward. His eyes were fixed in front of him, glassily staring, but, with what reason that was left to him, he suddenly realized where he was. He recognized the slopes before him, the horseshoe-shaped cluster of rocks. How well he remembered those rocks! He was on the edge of the quagmire!

His feet were already beginning to sink when, a creature bereft now of almost all reason, except a primitive sense of self preservation, he turned to the left and began to skirt the swamp.

Bert Johnson called, 'Better give in, Gaylord. You're trapped, you fool.'

Gaylord did not hear the words, though the sound of the voice echoed in his inflamed brain. He turned his head. The black horse was still there, the man. He raised his gun and fired.

The man leaned his body to one side and fired back. The slug hit Gaylord in the fleshy part of his leg. He screamed and fell to his knees. His gun was jerked out of his hand. It glittered mockingly as it spun in the air, then it hit the oozy green slime. It sank immediately.

Gaylord remained on all fours. He was like a child fascinated by what he had watched, by the pretty green expanse, shifting and glittering in the sunshine, which he now saw before him. But the hoofbeats seemed to shake the very ground beneath him so he could not help but turn. The black horse was almost on top of him, the man was shouting.

Gaylord rose and, like a bird with a broken wing, flung himself forward.

'Come back, you fool!' yelled Johnson.

But the impetus of Gaylord's rush had already carried him into the middle of the quagmire. By that time he was in up to his knees and could get no further forward.

He began to sink quickly then and to scream.

He writhed around and his eyes, as they looked at the man standing on the bank, were insane. He waved his arms above his head and began to laugh.

Johnson grabbed the lariat from his saddle-pommel, shook out the loop and flung it. Gaylord was writhing about in the sucking grip of the mud and his arms were threshing. It was almost as if he fought the coil of rope away. His laughter rang out as if he was overjoyed at the huge joke.

The loop fell in a hopeless coil beside him. Johnson began to draw it back.

The laughter echoed and re-echoed. The hills flung the sound about as if sporting with it and finally tossed it back to its source where it was taken up by the madman, redoubled, and thrown again to the rocky sun-washed slopes.

Gaylord's shoulders were going under. He had dropped his arms and was dappling them in the mud as he laughed.

Johnson drew his gun, levelled it, and fired twice. Then he turned away and remounted his horse.

He did not once look back as he rode away. There was a film of unutterable weariness over his light-blue eyes and his smooth face seemed to have sagged and grown suddenly old. At last something was beginning to break through that inhuman crust.

He was a man struggling with his thoughts as he rode.

FOURTEEN

Little tubby Doc Gruber, crossing the yard in the sunshine, was accosted by a dirty, weary-looking young man. In answer to the young man's question he said: 'The Old Man will live, but he'll be paralysed from the waist downwards. A terrible thing for a man like him.' The doctor continued to shake his head wordlessly for a moment then he went on: 'I dug the slug out of the other man's shoulder. No bones broken. He's sleepin' now in the bunkhouse.'

'Thanks, doc.'

'Don't mention it,' said Gruber. Something he saw in the young man's eyes gave him a sudden feeling of compassion. Almost unconsciously he rested a hand for a moment on a broad shoulder. Then he passed on.

The young man went to the bunkhouse and opened the door. He almost collided with a wizened little fellow with his arm in a sling. It was Shorty Mann, the person who had been the first to welcome the man who had called himself Bert Johnson to the Curly Bar 6 territory. It had been an unconventional welcome but, though only a short time had passed since, had already

149

been forgotten. So much had happened. So very much!

Shorty said: 'Howdy, Bert.' His face was friendly. It was good to look upon.

He jerked a thumb. 'Your pard's taken my place.'

In the bunk recently occupied by the wounded little ranny Steve Lasare was lying. He was snoring like a pig.

After Shorty had passed him Bert Johnson stood uncertainly on the threshold of the bunkhouse like a child who had lost his bearings. He whirled at the sound of footsteps behind him.

'The Ol' Man's askin' for you,' said Slim Grady.

Johnson turned about and followed the lean young ramrod. Slim led him into the ranch house and through the dusty gloom of the hall to a back room.

'We got his bed down here,' he said. 'He wanted it that way.'

Johnson entered the room and came face to face with Luella. Her face was frozen, there was no hint of coquetry in it now, it was like that of a frightened child. She did not greet him. Her eyes went past him, to Slim. They were appealing.

Behind her was the bed, the body flat beneath the clothes, the craggy face out-jutting.

The Old Man's voice said: 'Is that Bert?'

'It is,' said Slim.

'Come over here, Bert.'

As Johnson crossed the room the Old Man went on: 'Take Luella outside, Slim. Then come back.'

'Dad—'

'Do as I say, Luella.'

Johnson stood uncertainly in the middle of the floor,

looking around him. He was like a sheepish child. Slim put his arm gently around the girl's shoulders and led her from the room.

'Come closer, Bert,' said the Old Man.

Johnson moved again. As he reached the side of the bed Slim re-entered the room. Johnson looked down into the Old Man's face. It was pale and composed; the lines seemed etched less deeply; the eyes did not smoulder, they were almost peaceful. The Old Man said: 'You got Gaylord.' It was half a question, half a statement.

'I got him,' said Johnson.

'It was him an' his dumb side-kick killed those men o' mine.'

'Ain't much doubt about that. George was like a dog at his master's heels all the time. More scared than any dog.'

'George was probably the only person who ever took Gaylord really seriously,' said the Old Man. 'Pore Gaylord.'

'It ain't like you to be so tolerant,' said Johnson.

'No, it isn't, is it?' The Old Man spoke half to himself. Then his voice strengthened as he went on a new tack. But the question was almost childish.

'Why would Gaylord want to do that to me an' my men?'

'I cain't answer that properly. You should be able to answer that better than me.'

'Yes,' said the Old Man. 'He allus hated me.'

'He was crazy-mad,' said Johnson. 'You represented the power he desired but had never had . . .'

'He tried to buy the ranch off'n me once,' went on the

151

Old Man as if the other had not spoken. He gave a sudden spurt of harsh laughter which made him cough. When the spasm had subsided he said: 'Imagine that, Bert, he tried to buy my ranch off'n me. You can understand what this ranch means to me, cain't you? . . .'

'I don't know.'

'I threw him off the place – the jumped-up jackass.'

'He thought if he could scare your men off, kill you or scare you off too, maybe somehow he could get hold of some of the territory round here . . .'

'First of all I thought it was Ep Browning. He hated me—'

'You made yourself hated. Whatever you've wanted you've taken. You haven't worried about whoever got hurt. You've crushed anything or anybody who got in your way—'

'You're right, Bert,' said the Old Man softly. 'No wonder they all hated me. I've tried to be different these last few years but I don't think it's been much good. You hate me, don't you, Bert?'

'I don't hate anybody now. I'm all finished with hatin'.'

'But you came here to kill me.'

'Yes, I came here to kill you.'

Slim Grady started forward from the foot of the bed.

'Stay where you are, Slim,' said the Old Man. His voice was suddenly resonant. The eyes that looked up at Johnson had regained some of their old smouldering fire. 'You've got a gun, Bert. I'm helpless an' Slim is unarmed. Kill me now – put me out of my misery, maybe that'd be the best way. Or maybe your revenge is sweeter the other way, just to watch me lie here help-less. I shall be like this till I'm finished, so the doc says.'

'Either way suits me,' said Johnson. 'You can't ride me.' He was the old Johnson. His face was set, his voice utterly devoid of expression.

'I forgot,' went on the Old Man. 'Slim says if it hadn't been for you I might've died back there on the trail. I'm indebted to you. Or am I? Maybe you couldn't pluck up enough courage to kill me back there on the trail. Can you do it now. . . ? Go on, draw your gun an' shoot me. Put me out of my misery—'

'Don't talk like that, boss,' burst out Slim.

'All right, Slim,' said the Old Man. 'Come closer will you? I want my prospective son-in-law to hear what I've got to say now. After he's heard it he might not want to be my son-in-law.'

'Boss, I—'

'Shut up. Come here.'

Finally Johnson and Slim stood side by side. The Old Man said: 'Slim, I want you to meet my nephew, Herbert Summerson, my brother's child. He came here to kill me because years and years ago, when he was a little shaver not old enough to understand a thing, I killed his father.' He paused as if expecting some reac-tion. But the two young men remained as if frozen. He went on: 'Yes, I killed my own brother. I'm not proud of it; strange as it may seem, I've suffered hell for it since. But it was him or me, he was the hellion in those days, he would've killed me. I just happened to be a little quicker on the draw that's all. Shall I tell you what the fight was about, Bert – the real reason for it?'

Johnson did not answer the question. He only said: 'How did you know who I was?'

'I didn't at first. Then as I watched you an' came to know you better I knew you couldn't be anybody else. You act like he used to, you walk the same, your eyes look the same – only his useter blaze more. He was a ringtailed little bobcat.' The Old Man's voice suddenly rose. 'I thought the world of him. Do you understand? – although I killed him I loved him. I loved him more than anything, than anybody . . . than my own wife . . .' His voice dropped to a whisper.

'And it was because of my wife that I killed him. She loved him too, more than she loved me. We quarrelled over her . . .'

Johnson leaned forward, his face worked. 'Is that true?'

'It's true all right. My wife took him away from your mother. I killed him. No wonder she hated us, an' no wonder she instilled that hate in her only child.'

'She's dead now,' said Johnson dully.

'I'm sorry,' said the Old Man. 'I hope her hate has not been carried on for her.'

'No more,' said Johnson. It was as if he was talking to himself. 'I've carried it with me for a good many years. It's made me strive to be better than any man, so that when the time came for me to do what I meant to do nothing would happen that I could not handle.' He gave a jerky laugh. 'I did not figure that somebody would get in in front o' me – a crazy bushwhacker who potted men like clay pigeons.'

The Old Man's hand came out of the bedclothes and rested on the young man's arm. His voice was almost happy as he said: 'Don't let it throw yuh, son. Never let anythin' throw yuh.'

And looking down at him, seeing the courage which shone in those eyes, a sudden peace stole over the young man. Inarticulately, he turned away.

It was a sunny gentle morning. A gentle time. Two riders rode away from a bunch of men outside the bunkhouse of the Curly Bar 6 who waved their hands and yelled after them.

The two riders passed in front of the ranch house and, as they did so, Luella and Slim came down the steps. The riders halted.

Slim said: 'How's the shoulder now, Steve?'

The little tubby man with the luxurious black moustache and his arm in a sling said: 'It's fine. Bert's the dandiest little nurse you ever did see.'

Beside him, Bert grinned and said: 'I've had to stand for his joshin' far too long. I'm gettin' that arm fixed up jest fine an' dandy so I can meet him on an equal footing.'

The man and the girl laughed. The man said: 'Guess this is *adios* then?'

'Yeh,' said Bert. 'We're goin' back to our old territory. But don't worry, we'll get over agin for the wedding.'

Slim came closer and shook hands with both of them. Luella followed suit.

She looked up at Bert and said: 'You'll keep your promise?'

For a moment he was the old Johnson again as he answered gravely: 'I'll keep my promise.'

Then he grinned and she stepped aside and with a

flip of his hand he rode past her. Steve and he rode around the back of the ranch house, their horses' hoofs thundering on the hard sod. Before they set out across the range they looked back. In a lower rear window an arm was raised and waved slowly. Although they knew the Old Man could not raise himself to see them, they saluted him with a flourish before they passed on.